OTHER YEARLING BOOKS BY PHYLLIS REYNOLDS NAYLOR
YOU WILL ENJOY:

THE AGONY OF ALICE
ALICE IN RAPTURE, SORT OF
ALL BECAUSE I'M OLDER
BEETLES, LIGHTLY TOASTED
MAUDIE IN THE MIDDLE
NIGHT CRY
ONE OF THE THIRD GRADE THONKERS
THE WITCH HERSELF
WITCH WATER
WITCH'S SISTER

YEARLING BOOKS/YOUNG YEARLINGS/YEARLING CLASSICS are designed especially to entertain and enlighten young people. Patricia Reilly Giff, consultant to this series, received her bachelor's degree from Marymount College and a master's degree in history from St. John's University. She holds a Professional Diploma in Reading and a Doctorate of Humane Letters from Hofstra University. She was a teacher and reading consultant for many years, and is the author of numerous books for young readers.

For a complete listing of all Yearling titles,
write to Dell Readers Service
P.O. Box 1045
South Holland, IL 60473

TO WALK
THE
SKY PATH

Phyllis Reynolds Naylor

A Yearling Book

To Forrest Keith

Published by
Dell Publishing
a division of
Bantam Doubleday Dell Publishing Group, Inc.
666 Fifth Avenue
New York, New York 10103

ISBN: 0-440-40636-6

Reprinted by arrangement with the author

Printed in the United States of America

June 1992

10 9 8 7 6 5 4 3 2

OPM

One

LIKE a king snake slithering up from the south, the wind rippled the saw grass. Farther on, in the mangrove swamps, twisted roots of moss-covered trees rose up from the water to be a part of the forest above. It was here in the camp that Billie waited, listening for the sound of his uncle's airboat, scanning the darkening sky for the red star, first of the evening. This was the night to go frogging.

"Owaci kidisci," old Abraham said, pointing to the evening star now visible above a distant cypress tree. "It rises whether we watch or not." It was the signal to put away the toy canoes and tomahawks he

was carving, to rest in the peace of the evening. He smiled, nearly toothless, and leaned his elbows on his wrinkled knees as he sat cross-legged on the wooden platform.

"You can just make out the Milky Way," Billie Tommie said, and lay flat on his back beside his grandfather. "See? There, and all along there. Sometimes it's dim and sometimes it's bright. Why is that?"

Old Abraham nodded and watched with clouded eyes as though—even in his eightieth year—he had never lost the wonder of it. "It is bright at the death of a good man, Billie. I hope it shines for me, to light my path to the city in the sky." He spoke in the sing-song dialect of the Mikasuki tongue. Grandfather understood English, but could not speak it himself. So when Billie talked with him, he spoke Mikasuki too.

"Doesn't it shine for everybody?" Billie asked.

"Only for a man who is liked by all, who does not talk in an evil manner. For a brave man, who does not lie or steal. Only he can cross the bridge of stars."

"What if a man is bad?" Billie wanted to know. "The light just goes out and the guy gets lost up there?"

Abraham grunted at the ignorance of his grandson and looked at him dolefully. Didn't Mush Jim teach him anything? That was an uncle's job. People just didn't keep to the old ways anymore.

"The bad man, he stays in the ground. If you go into the woods and step where the bad person is

6

hidden, you feel afraid, even though the grave is covered with bushes and trees. You know evil is there."

The goose bumps rose on Billie's arms. Somehow he'd thought that by the time he was twelve, he wouldn't be afraid of anything any longer. That is the age a Seminole boy becomes a man, and Billie had only two more years to wait. Now he wasn't sure. Maybe fear would be part of him all his life. Then he was conscious of the old man's quiet.

"The stars will shine for you, Grandfather," he said fondly. "I know it. But it will be a long time yet. Seminoles live longer than almost anybody. Remember the woman who lived to be a hundred and twenty? You're healthy as a big turtle."

Abraham was pleased. "Yes, I am strong for my years. Only the greatest storm can knock me down."

This time it was Billie's turn to be quiet. Of all the Mikasuki Seminoles, Abraham seemed the most thoroughly Indian to Billie. The stars would shine for Grandfather, he was sure. But would they shine for him? When he was here in the camp, he felt very much like Abraham. But sometimes when he was in school, he almost forgot he had been born a Mikasuki. Tonight, however, Billie was Indian.

A Gulf breeze swept through the Everglades, rustling the palmetto thatching on the roofs of the chickees—the huts which formed the four corners of the camp. There were no walls to the chickees. Each hut was a wooden platform three feet off the ground, where the family sat or slept, with posts holding up the roof.

In the cookhouse, Billie's mother and grandmother squatted by the fire, patiently tending the evening meal. There was no platform in this chickee, but bare ground for the floor. The delicious fragrance of chicken and sweet potatoes filled the air, mingling with the damp smell of the earth.

There were islands all through the marshy forest—shell mounds, the natives called them—which rose up above the murky water. It was on this particular island that the Tommie family had their home: three chickees for sleeping, one for cooking, and a little garden plot where Alice Tommie, Billie's mother, grew beans, corn, tomatoes, and pumpkins. A few pigs and chickens wandered about, rooting in the damp shade beneath the huts or scratching in the dirt.

Watsie, Billie's small sister, whined for food, and Grandmother dipped a biscuit in grease and handed it to her. Grandmother, whose name was Sihoki, was sixty-seven, but twice as heavy as Grandfather, and the many strands of beads around her neck made her appear larger still. She raised herself to a bench beside the cooking grate, her colorful skirt spread out around her, and lifted Watsie onto her lap. It was a good time in the camp when work was over, dinner was cooking, and the men were coming home. It was the hour Sihoki liked best.

A noise far off in the distance made the family's dog sit up. Billie swung his legs over the side of the platform, listening. The noise grew louder and louder, ripping the stillness. It was the deafening roar of Mush Jim's airboat, propelled by an airplane engine. By the time the airboat reached the north side of the island, the roar drowned out all other sound. Suddenly the motor cut off, the dog stopped barking, and the Everglades was still as moonlight.

Billie Tommie ran to the bank where his father and brother were climbing out of the boat. Mush Jim, his uncle, picked up his lunch bucket and followed them up the path.

"Mr. Miller comes tomorrow," Billie reminded his brother, Charlie. "Want to go frogging with me?" They hadn't been at the business long, and Billie wanted to keep the trader coming.

Charlie was tired, but he said, "Sure. If we don't have any frogs, he may not come again." He reached forward and grabbed a root of the big cypress to help himself up the bank. Billie followed behind, noticing the weary slump of his brother's shoulders. Charlie was only thirteen, but already he did the work of a man.

"We wouldn't have to go, Charlie," Billie said suddenly. "Grandfather and I caught garfish today, and I scaled them. Got two cups of scales. Mr. Miller said he'd buy those too. He can sell them to a necklace factory for us. We could tell him we'll have frogs again next week."

Charlie turned around and smiled faintly. "And the frogs would laugh because they got away. No, we will go gigging tonight."

From the back, the brothers looked almost alike,

9

except that Charlie was taller. Both were slender like their father, with narrow shoulders and long arms. But their faces were very different. Charlie resembled his father—high forehead, straight nose, and thick, black wavy hair. Billie looked more like his uncle, Mush Jim, for his head was round, his cheek bones prominent, and his hair was a dark reddish-brown. When Billie was happy, his lips stretched wide, showing his teeth. But Charlie's mouth hardly moved at all. He smiled with his eyes, and sometimes only the family could tell he was happy.

When the little group reached the cookhouse, Mush Jim dropped his lunch bucket and sat down to take off his boots. Tiger, Billie's father, was too tired even for that. He lay back on the bare ground, his eyes narrow slits as he turned his face up to the thatch above him. Two-year-old Watsie crawled over and leaned against his arm, nibbling her biscuit, and the camp was quiet now so the men could rest.

Like brilliant tropical birds, Mother and Grandmother moved noiselessly about preparing supper in the unique costumes of the Seminoles. Their skirts were bands of different colored materials stitched together, and thin, waist-long capes covered their shoulders. Grandmother's neck was hidden by layers and layers of beads, and she wore her black hair in a high pompadour. Alice Tommie, already becoming plump like Sihoki, wore only half as many beads and styled her hair in a knot above her forehead. Grandfather, too, wore the traditional long shirt and kerchief of the older Seminole men. But Tiger and Mush Jim and Charlie and Billie dressed in blue jeans and boots unless they wanted to look especially nice. Then they put on their homemade jackets of many stripes and colors.

There was talk of alligators at the evening meal, especially of the alligator called the Big One. Mush Jim had seen him once, and so had some of the other Indians along the canal.

"Too mean to handle, that's what," Mush Jim said, tearing the meat off the chicken bone in his hand and stuffing it in his mouth. "The rangers want to put it on a 'gator farm where it can't bother anybody. But they have to catch him first, and the Big One's old and smart." Everyone spoke the Mikasuki language when they were together so that the women, too, could understand. Many years before, when Tiger and Mush Jim had taken jobs outside the camp, they had learned English, but it was nice at the end of the day to come home and speak the language they knew so well. When he talked alone with his nephews, however, Mush Jim usually spoke English. He wanted them to learn it well, and now English came as easily to Billie as Mikasuki, and Charlie, too, spoke it well.

Sihoki waddled across to Abraham and put a pail of gruel and a *sofkee* spoon beside him, turning her toes in as she walked to keep from stepping on her skirt. Then she crouched down, breaking his chicken into small pieces so that he could swallow it without needing to chew.

"What's the Big One done, Mush Jim?" Billie asked.

"Ralph Jumper said it killed four other 'gators in

11

one night over his way. And it ate Beets Fraser's dog. Fraser saw it. The 'gator tossed it this way and that. Swallowed it down in three big gulps and then started for Beets himself. Fraser says if he'd had his gun, he'd have shot it, law or no."

Old Abraham sucked the gruel into his dark toothless mouth. "I have seen them as long as a chickee and as fierce as a wildcat," he murmured. "As fast as the wind!"

"Be careful when you're gigging," Tiger reminded his sons, reaching across Billie for another biscuit. "If he's as bold as they say, you'll meet him sooner or later."

The moon was bright on the water as Billie and Charlie stepped into the airboat. The beam from the hunting lantern scanned the surface. Like taillights of automobiles in the distance, pairs of orange-red coals caught in the beam, moving slowly across the water. The red eyes, Billie knew, belonged to the adult male alligators, while the greenish-yellow belonged to the females and the young.

The night animals were out, and the noises were different now from the sounds of the day. The alligators were on the prowl for food. So were the deer and wildcat, the fox and puma. The sharp blades of grass made a metallic sound in the soft breeze, and from somewhere close by came the terrified death-squeal of a marsh rabbit. A bullfrog sang out a throaty *kà-chug* from one bank and was answered from another. The thicket rustled and snapped as raccoons and water rats scurried along the banks.

With an explosive roar, the motor caught and held, and the airboat vibrated with the intensity of the noise. Instantly the pairs of red and yellow eyes all over the swamp submerged, and the airboat drowned out all the night sounds that were left. In many places the water was only two inches deep, but out in the lagoon it sometimes went as deep as nine feet. Skimming along the edge of the marsh, where the tangled moss hung down to the ground, Billie turned his head from one side to the other as the beam of the lantern scanned the logs and the bank and the water.

The frogs were there in the favorite hunting place, a tangle of rocks and decaying logs. Otters, lizards, and soft-shell turtles also came sometimes to play. Charlie slowed the motor till the boat was barely moving. Swiftly the boys stood up, keeping the lantern's strong beam focused on the half dozen frogs which sat in the water, dazed from the intensity of the light. Taking their three-pronged spears in hand, they leaned over the side of the boat and noiselessly plunged them into the frogs. Swiftly they dropped their catch in the bucket, and the airboat cruised on down the water.

They did not talk as they worked, except to say, "There!" or "Now!" Billie enjoyed the adventure. It was a change from geography and spelling and arithmetic lessons. But to Charlie, already tired, it was one more job to be done, and once the bucket was full, they could go home.

It was slow work. Some nights there seemed to be more frogs than others, some seasons many, some seasons few. Mr. Miller would pay more for frog legs in the scant season; and the big restaurants in Miami, where he sold them, would raise the price on their menus.

They covered the lagoon, and slipped down the narrow canals which branched off further still into low alligator trails. Then they came back and did the lagoon again, but this time there were no more frogs in the favorite hunting spot. It was as though, in some mysterious way, the message had traveled up and down the canals and through the vast swamp that the boys were out with their spears, and the bullfrogs of the Everglades lay low.

Billie thought about it. Grandfather would have talked to the frogs and thanked them for allowing him to catch them. Charlie and Billie never did. Perhaps it was this rudeness that made the others disappear.

The bucket was only three-quarters full, but the boys decided to quit. When they got back to camp, Alice and Tiger were still up, talking in the cookhouse. Billie and Charlie sat down beside them and ate what was left in the stew pot.

"It was a long day for you, Charlie," Tiger said. "Now you work like a man." He turned to his wife. "All day he works the vegetable fields, and then he is out at night hunting frogs."

"There are other things he could be doing if we lived near the highway," Alice replied. "He would have friends like Billie does. Most of his friends have left the swamps. His cousins live on the reservation." She stopped and shook her head, then decided to say it anyway. "I wish we had sent him to school."

Charlie grinned quickly and shrugged. "I don't think I would have liked it," he said, and went on eating.

"Billie's the only one . . ." Mother continued, "the only one in this family who's been to school."

Billie didn't say anything. He liked school—most of it, at least. But it didn't seem right that he should have something Charlie didn't. It wasn't the Indian way. Once he brought his reader home and tried to teach the words to Charlie. But Charlie said the words just looked like possum tracks on paper, so he gave up.

It was too late now for more talking. Across the clearing, Mush Jim blew out his lantern and lay down. The boys went over to their chickee and took their bedrolls down from the rafters under the roof. They spread them out on the wooden platform and lowered the muslin canopies to keep out mosquitoes. Here they were safe off the ground from snakes, protected from insects, and lulled to sleep by the swishing sound of wind through the palmetto thatch.

There was a distant scream of a panther and the mocking *ka-chug* of all the bullfrogs which Billie and his brother hadn't caught. From the neighboring chickee came the sound of Sihoki's snoring, in syncopated timing with snorts from Abraham.

"Charlie," said Billie, "did you ever see the Big One?"

"Huh uh."

"Would you be scared if you did?"

There was no answer. Charlie was already asleep. Billie's thoughts jumped ahead to the following day—to the trader and the frogs and the restaurants in Miami. Suddenly he realized it would be Friday and he hadn't finished his paper about Thomas Jefferson and the Revolutionary War. Mrs. Kelly would ask him why, and he'd have to tell her he was out frogging. And then, as sleep closed in, he could almost hear what she was going to say.

Two

THE SKY was light long before sunrise. The chickees stood out starkly against a backdrop of scrub oak, solid with bed canopies which fluttered softly in the morning breeze. The dog slept in the dry ashes of the cook fire, but the hens were already scratching at the bare ground, and the rooster stretched his neck, calling good-morning to the night creatures who were just going to bed.

Sihoki awoke first, as usual. She lifted the edge of her canopy and peeped out, surveying the garden and the forest beyond, communicating with her small world before her work began. As she dressed, the canopy shook and billowed. When all was in order, she swung the canopy back over her head and crawled down. She twitched a string on the right, then on the left. The muslin canopy dropped, and she rolled it up and stuck it in the rafters.

Sihoki tottered on to the next chickee, shook Alice Tommie's canopy, and then went over to Mush Jim's. By the time the men had dressed, Mother and Grandmother were in the cookhouse, and garfish was baking in the ashes of the fire. Only Watsie remained asleep in her little hammock—a bath towel suspended between two ropes—and the dog, routed from the cookhouse, grudgingly plopped down beside her, not quite ready to run just yet.

Billie sat down on one of the logs of the star fire, arranged as spokes in a wheel. Flames burned at the center, and the logs were pushed forward as needed. Meanwhile, the far end of each log made a good seat for the family members when they ate together.

Mother slid a piece of fish and a fried biscuit onto Billie's tin plate. She was still thinking about Charlie and the possibility of moving to the other side of the lagoon nearer the highway.

"It wouldn't be just for Charlie," she said, taking up where she'd left off the night before. "It might be better for us all. Billie could walk to the school bus stop without waiting for Mush Jim to take him across in the boat. And Tiger would have his truck handy."

It was a subject she had brought up before, and this time Mush Jim spoke his mind on it too.

"Sure would make things easier for me. All this

travel back and forth takes time away from my job. If we're going to go to school and work on the other side, we might as well live there too. That's how I see it."

"We could buy a trailer," Mother added. "We could even build a cinder-block house with lights and a sink."

There was quiet as they waited for Sihoki to speak. It was her clan, her camp, and she had the final say.

"I'm too old to learn housekeeping," she said at last, and that was that.

As Billie sped over the water in the airboat, between his father and Charlie, and Mush Jim on the high seat above them, he thought about what his mother had said. It had never occurred to him that they would ever leave the far island, even though most of the Seminoles had left the swamps long ago. But usually, when this happened, grandmothers agreed and went along too.

Though Alice had become a Tommie, taking her husband's last name when she married, she remained a member of her mother's clan—the Wind Clan—and so did all her children. Among the Seminoles, a married daughter usually stays in her mother's camp with her husband and children and also the unmarried sons and daughters.

Billie tried to remember as far back as he could. They had lived in one other camp before this one, but as the posts began to rot and the roof came apart, it was easier to build new chickees somewhere else than to repair the old ones. So they had moved to their present island. They had always lived on the far side of the swamp, however, across the lagoon, away from the tourists and the noise of their automobiles. He could not imagine how it would be living closer to the highway. And it was simply unthinkable for the rest of the family to go, leaving Abraham and Sihoki behind. Grandfather was to the family what fire was on a cold morning, what rain was in a dry season, what stars were on a dark night.

The motor quit abruptly, and the boat moved in toward the dock. Tiger got out, followed by Charlie and Billie. Mush Jim picked up the bucket of frog legs and the scales from the garfish and took them to the little shack where the sign, "Air Boat Rides: Low Rates," hung askew above the door.

An old pickup truck was parked by the shack. Charlie and Tiger got in and, with a wave to Billie, started off down the Tamiami Trail, the highway which stretched from Tampa to Miami. Charlie would get out first and catch a ride on another truck which would take him to the vegetable fields. Tiger would go to work with a highway construction crew farther on.

Billie stuck his hands in his pockets, the full sleeves of his bright-colored shirt blowing in the morning breeze. Far down the highway he could see the yellow bus coming, and wondered if he could finish the Revolutionary War on the ride to school.

He took a seat to himself and opened his tablet, resting it on his knee.

"The reason there was trouble between the colonists and the British was..." he had written halfway down the page. He started to finish the sentence, when a brown-haired boy in jeans got on at the next stop and slid in beside him.

"Hi," said Jeffrey Miller, grinning. "See you're still at it."

Billie knew he wouldn't get it done now. Jeffrey was a big talker, but Billie liked him anyway. He smiled back, all teeth.

"It's only half finished," he told his friend. "Mrs. Kelly will really be mad."

"Why?"

"Because I went fishing with Grandfather instead. And last night I went gigging for frogs."

"Don't tell her that, then. Tell her your grandfather needed you—that you had to work."

"But I really didn't have to," Billie confessed. "I just wanted to. Sometimes Abraham needs company."

"Well, it's half true, then."

"Half true is even worse than lying," Billie said.

Jeffrey gave a whistle and slid down despairingly in his seat.

"Man! I'll never understand you! How can half-bad be worse than all-bad?"

It seemed so simple to Billie. "Because, if a person mixes true things together with lies, he's being tricky, and it is harder to get to the truth. Mush Jim says it is sometimes easier to deal with a bad man because then you know what to expect."

Jeffrey stared at Billie a moment, trying to understand. "You sure know how to make trouble for yourself," he said at last. "Anyway, did you catch some frogs? Isn't this the day my dad picks them up?"

Billie nodded. The bus pulled up in front of the school, and the boys and girls got out.

Mrs. Kelly stood straight and stiff in front of the classroom like a statue at the public library.

"You may turn in your history papers and then get right to work on your math assignment. There will be a special science movie later this morning, and Mr. Bernard has asked that you come early."

Billie kept his eyes on his desk as the others shuffled up to the front of the room. But Mrs. Kelly was watching.

"Billie Tommie?" she said. "Your paper, please?"

"I didn't finish it," he said numbly.

"Why not?"

Jeff sidled past him as he returned to his own seat. "Your *grandfather*, dope. Say he needed you!"

"I . . . went fishing . . . with my grandfather," Billie said.

Mrs. Kelly acted as though she hadn't heard right. "You were fishing from the time you got home until the time you went to bed?"

"No, after it got dark I went frogging with Charlie."

Some of the children laughed out loud, but it was friendly laughter. They liked Billie.

"Billie," said Mrs. Kelly. "Do you think that this is a proper excuse for not doing your homework?"

"No," Billie answered. "But Grandfather thinks it is."

"Did he realize that he was keeping you from your studies?"

"No. He thought he was teaching me something."

The children laughed again, and Billie was embarrassed.

"That will do," said Mrs. Kelly. "Work on it over the weekend, Billie, and turn your paper in Monday. I'll have to lower your grade, of course."

As the morning wore on, Billie stole glances at his teacher. What was it that made it so hard for him to get along with her? She wasn't really mean. It was just. . . . He rested his chin in his hands and thought about it. She acted as though she had to keep after him all the time or he'd fail the whole fifth grade. But wasn't he doing well? He got mostly B's, some C's, and even A's in science and art. Was that so bad?

At ten-thirty, Mrs. Kelly sent everyone to the science room down the hall, and Billie was glad to go. As he started through the doorway, however, the teacher called him back. She waited until all the children were out of the room. Then she looked at him sorrowfully, as though she really wanted to understand, but couldn't.

"Billie," she said, "you have a big responsibility, you know. You're the only one of your family who's ever been to school. Isn't that what you told me?"

"Yes," he mumbled, wishing now that he hadn't told her.

"I want to see you educated, Billie. I want you to

have a chance to get a good job later on. You don't want to live in a chickee the rest of your life, do you?"

Billie stared at her. Why not? What was wrong with that?

She took a deep breath and tried again. "Don't you want your parents to be proud of you?"

"But they are."

"I mean *real* proud—proud to see you do something maybe no other Seminole Indian had ever done. Get the best grades in school—the best job?"

Billie shook his head. "They wouldn't be proud of that," he told her earnestly. "Not if I tried to do better than everybody else. And Charlie—I'd feel bad about Charlie."

She sat there shaking her head as though she couldn't comprehend any more. "You'd better go," she said finally. "You'll be late."

Billie picked up his notebook and started down the hall. Better not tell Grandfather what Mrs. Kelly had in mind, he decided. To do something no other Indian had ever done? Be better than them all? Nobody ever walked the sky path for that. His family was proud of him just because he was Seminole, because he tried to be a good Mikasuki—as good as all the rest. What kind of pride did white people have, that they had to top somebody else to be important? Now it was Billie who didn't understand.

Mr. Bernard had just turned on the projector. A movie about reptiles and amphibians flashed on the screen.

"Glad you're here, Billie," he said when he saw him dive in a seat near the back. "We may need to ask you some questions when it's over."

It was a good movie. If he ever got a white man's job, Billie told himself, it would be something to do with animals—a zoo keeper, maybe, or a man who studied fish in a laboratory. Perhaps he'd even teach science in school like Mr. Bernard. He liked to draw too, though. Maybe he'd be an artist who painted birds and animals.

When the light came on afterwards, the teacher said, "The movie told us a few things about alligators and crocodiles, but it didn't say how to tell them apart. Did anybody notice from the pictures?"

No one raised his hand.

"Billie?"

Billie didn't like being the one who knew something that no one else did. But he'd do it for Mr. Bernard.

"The crocodile's snout is pointed, and its skin is sort of bumpy. The alligator has a round snout, and its skin looks like little squares."

"That's good, Billie. Exactly right." Mr. Bernard faced the class again. "So the next time any of you kids go swimming and something grabs you, at least you'll be able to tell which it is before you go under."

They all laughed. Billie, too.

The September sun was intense, and heat shimmered up from the highway as Billie trudged back to Mush Jim's boat shack. The noise of the school bus grew fainter and fainter. He took off his bright shirt which Grandmother had made, and continued on in his tee shirt. In a few hours the sun would be down, and the Florida night would be breezy and cool. Then the mosquitoes would be everywhere. He'd need the long sleeves then.

Mush Jim's shack was on the south side of the Tamiami Trail, perched on the edge of the canal which ran alongside the highway for miles and miles. There was a little dirt parking lot where the tourists pulled in. Perhaps twice a day—more in the tourist season—Mush Jim would take a boat full of tourists for a ride in his airboat for three dollars apiece.

Mush Jim felt good about people who stopped, though Billie sometimes didn't like them. Mush Jim said that if somebody was willing to pass up the slick boat rides all along the road, with their lighted signs and gravel parking lots and alligator pens, and come to his instead, then they were entitled to something extra. And so he gave the longest airboat rides of anybody else on the Tamiami Trail.

He would take his boat load down the canal to the open place leading to the low-lying marsh. Zigzagging through the patches of swamp grass that looked like thousands of islands stretched over a vast lake, he would roar toward the mangrove swamp, the nose of the airboat rising up off the water as though the flat-bottomed craft were ready to fly. Children, if there were any along, put their hands over their ears and screamed with excitement.

Billie's uncle guided the boat this way and that, and the stern would swing around first, the bow following. Then they would reach the swamp where the trees and moss seemed one with the water. Here, in the mysterious, narrow waterways, which were always in shade, Mush Jim steered his wide-eyed customers, cutting the motor so that he could point out the snakes and other wildlife they might see along the way, and telling the Indian legends he had heard from old Abraham, his father. On, deeper and deeper into the Everglades he went until he knew by the smiles on their faces that they were pleased with the trip. But he never took them close to the far island and the family camp. Sihoki wanted no tourists looking in her cooking pot.

Sometimes, but not often, Mush Jim did not take the airboat out at all. Sometimes when Billie came back from school he found his uncle asleep, smelling of whiskey. If Mush Jim ever got angry with the tourists, he never showed it. If they insulted him or tried to cheat him out of a dollar, he remained polite and smiling. But sometimes the strain was too much, and Mush Jim drank himself into a stupor. Then Billie would have to wait till his father drove up, and together with Charlie, they would lift Mush Jim into the airboat and take him back to the island. Tiger did not drink, but he did not speak ill of his brother-in-law.

"Let him be," he would tell his sons as they laid Mush Jim down in the chickee. "Tomorrow's problems come soon enough."

On this day Mush Jim was repainting his sign in big red letters against a white background.

"You look hot," he said. "I left a Coke inside for you."

Billie went into the shack and got the Coke from the small table, then came out. "Did Mr. Miller come for the frogs?"

"Yes. And he took the garfish scales too. Said he'd stop every Friday on his way to Miami if we wanted him to."

Billie squatted down in the shade, resting his weight on his ankles. "Were you ever a soldier in a war?" he asked suddenly.

"Nope. Tried to enlist in the Korean War, but they wouldn't take me."

"How come?"

" 'Cause I couldn't read or write."

Billie looked puzzled. "But you can now."

"Took a night school class to learn it, that's why. By the time I learned, the war was over."

"Were you sorry?"

"I was then, but not now. Think I can do a lot more for my people right here than blowing off somebody's head across the ocean." He dipped his brush in the paint and looked at Billie. "Why? You thinking of being a soldier?"

"No. I've got to finish a paper on Thomas Jefferson and the Revolutionary War, that's all. I might decide to be a science teacher or something."

"Think you could make it—high school and then college?"

"I'd sure try. If I had the money."

This time Mush Jim put the brush down and looked him square in the face. "If you make up your mind to do it, Billie, we'll find the money somewhere. There's places to borrow, and scholarships we could try. Whatever it takes to get you a good job, that's what we'll do—Tiger and Alice and me. But you got to do the best you can at school right now."

That meant getting his homework done, garfish or no garfish, Billie thought. He pulled out his tablet and sat in the shade to work his math problems while Mush Jim finished painting the sign.

It was hard to concentrate, however. Billie was more interested in the careful way Mush Jim lettered his sign, tipping the brush on edge so he could paint a fine line. In some ways Mush Jim and Grandfather had similar ideas about getting along in the world, and in others they were very different. Mush Jim was just as proud of being Mikasuki as Grandfather, for this was the only tribe in the country which never surrendered and never signed a peace treaty. Mush Jim, Billie knew, would never even move to a government reservation. The Tommies had always been independent, and wished to stay that way.

At the same time, however, Mush Jim wanted a better life for the family. He wanted to make work easier for Sihoki, his mother, and Alice, his sister. He wanted the children to be educated. He wanted a business that would provide enough money so that they would be dependent on no one. He was becoming wise in the ways of the white businessmen,

and he wanted to learn all he could without giving up
a bit of his Seminole heritage.

But Grandfather . . . Billie put down his pencil
and smiled when he thought of the old man and
how different he was. Abraham saw nothing useful
at all in the white man's world. To Grandfather,
progress meant cutting down acres and acres of
century-old trees, changing the character of the
forests, disturbing the wildlife, and polluting the
rivers and streams. All that a Mikasuki needed to
know, he said, he could learn on the far island, and
if a man spent his life observing the animals and
the seasons and the stars, he would still learn only a
fraction of what they had to teach him.

When the pickup truck pulled in later, Billie
had finished his math problems. He climbed into the
boat beside his father, and Mush Jim started the
engine. Charlie was tired and fell asleep with his
head resting against the legs of Mush Jim's high
seat, mouth open, oblivious to the roar of the motor.

But Tiger leaned forward, his brown arms on his
knees, eyes squinting wearily out over the water,
tired shoulders hunched beneath his torn shirt, the
thin creases of fatigue in his face.

Billie watched him while the boat moved south
toward the mangrove trees. "The silent one," Sihoki
once called her son-in-law, and it was a good name,
for Tiger was the quietest one of them all. Maybe that
was the way it was when a man left his own relatives
and went to live with a wife and her clan. Maybe he
always felt a little apart, a stranger.

Of the three men in the camp, Billie felt he knew his father the least. Tiger rarely spoke about his feelings. He got up and went to work and came home and went to bed. He did what had to be done to make a living for his family; and what he thought about being a Seminole and working on the white man's roads, he kept to himself. It was as if he had given up long ago, and Billie felt a special pang when he thought of his father. This feeling made him want to have a say in his own life, whatever he did with it.

Abraham came down to the water to meet them, holding Watsie by the hand, his face in a toothless smile. When the motor cut off and the dog stopped barking, he said to Billie, "You come late today. We could not fish."

"I had homework to do, Grandfather, and Mush Jim was painting, so we just stayed on the other side and worked."

The old man shook his head. "I do not understand school. You study when you are there. You study when you are not there. When is there time for the fish?"

"It's rough." Billie grinned. "That's what I tried to tell Mrs. Kelly, but I don't think I got through."

There was a small well beyond the garden, and Billie went to get a drink. Abraham sat down on a log beside the rows of collard greens and beans and tomatoes and watched his grandson, glad that he was home. Behind them, the pigs ran wild in the swamp, and a flock of yellow-headed, red-cheeked buzzards feasted on a carcass in the distance.

"The teacher—she wants you to learn all there is in one day?" Grandfather asked quizzically.

Billie laughed, splashing his face with water and wiping his sleeve across it. "Seems that way sometimes. I don't think you'd like her, Grandfather. She's got to be busy every minute, never stops, hardly smiles even."

"For that I should feel sorry for her."

"Well, I sure don't. I don't like her, either. She acts as though I'm dumb. She always expects me to do something stupid, and thinks she's the only one who can save me."

Abraham fixed his eyes on Billie without blinking.

"You are an Indian, Billie. Long before there was a schoolhouse, there were Seminole. Long before there was a teacher, there were Seminole. Long before blackboards and books and study-every-night there were Seminole. This is our land and she is now upon it. Do not allow her to make you angry. Do not let her voice make you afraid. It is nothing more than the gobble of a turkey."

Billie sat down on the log beside Abraham. Wouldn't Mrs. Kelly blow up if she heard that— if the next time she chewed him out, he called her a turkey? Somehow, though, he felt stronger after talking with Grandfather. He always did. Grandfather, for all his frailty, was like a rock to hold on to when the earth was shaking.

They had just finished eating when they heard the odd noise. Just as the sky was turning purple over the strangler fig trees, there was a whine of a plane that sounded strangely low and somehow different.

Tiger had heard the sound before. "Listen," he said, tilting his ear to the sky.

The whine grew louder and louder, punctuated by sputtering and a dull chugging, grinding noise. When it sounded directly above them, they could make out a small plane, obviously in trouble, against the sky over the clearing.

"You think he'll bail out?" asked Charlie.

"More likely he'll try to land it," said Mush Jim. "No pilot wants to lose his plane unless he has to."

Alice Tommie shoved Watsie under the platform of the chickee in case the plane crashed into camp, and tried to hush the dog, who was barking frantically. The plane continued to circle above, its wings dipping lower and lower. The whine grew louder until it seemed it was almost upon them. Then there was a crashing sound of water and underbrush, a final chug, and silence.

Tiger and Mush Jim, with Charlie and Billie at their heels, hurried down the path to the airboat. But Sihoki stood by the cooking pot, spoon in hand. "Do not bring anyone here," she called. "Do not bring a stranger to this place."

Three

HE HAD heard of it happening before. When the old men got together at the Green Corn Dance or the family visited friends on Big Cypress, someone would tell about the plane crash of 1929, or the time a woman pilot was rescued. Something could go wrong with a plane motor over the Everglades as well as anyplace else, and when a small plane went down, it was often only the Indians who could find it.

It had always sounded exciting. But now, as the air-boat sped across the grassy marsh, Billie wished it hadn't happened. He thought of the pilot, and felt sick.

Mush Jim circled around the island, heading south, farther and farther from the Tamiami Trail, the only road that could carry them to a hospital if they needed it. Maybe they wouldn't. Perhaps the man was dead. Through canals and water trails barely wide enough for the boat to pass, they made their way. Tiger always said that if Mush Jim were dropped anywhere at all in the Everglades with a blindfold on, he'd find his way home in time for supper.

"What do you think, Mush Jim?" Tiger was asking now.

"I think it's due south," Mush Jim yelled back from his perch on the high seat. "The angle it was going, it wouldn't have dropped straight down."

"Nothing burning I can see," Tiger said, and they watched the sky for a column of smoke. "At least he's got that much going for him. But it makes him harder to find."

Charlie stood in the back of the boat, holding onto Mush Jim, collar turned up around his neck.

"There it is!" Charlie yelled above the roar of the motor, and pointed to the left.

Like a fallen bird, two white wings protruded from the muck. It was as though they had been there for an eternity. There was no movement, no sound. Only the smell of gasoline and the slick shine of oil on the surface of the water. Like quicksand, the Everglades could swallow up people, animals, and planes as well, slowly pulling them down beneath the thick surface. Tiger had seen several downed aircraft in his time, and there had been some he couldn't save.

The airboat swung around to the left side of the plane, and instantly Mush Jim was on one wing, yanking at the cabin door, Tiger beside him. It wouldn't budge. Picking up his tool kit, Mush Jim heaved it against the window full force, and the glass broke, drawing the muddy water inside.

Billy sucked in his breath. A man lay slumped on his side, one arm twisted grotesquely about his head. His shirt sleeve was soaked in blood, and one leg twitched strangely.

Tiger reached inside and closed his fingers around the man's wrist. "Alive," he said. He opened the door from the inside. Carefully, Tiger and Mush Jim worked to pull the pilot out. Inch by inch they dragged him, bracing his neck and back. Suddenly the man gave a strange cry, like an animal caught in a trap.

"Lungs are strong," Tiger said, encouraged by the sound.

As they lifted him from the plane and placed him in the airboat, he cried out again.

"It's the only way," Mush Jim said. "We've got to get you out. We'll make it, now. Hold on."

"My arm!" the man cried again, and blood ran down his elbow and dripped on the floor of the boat.

He was about Tiger's age, with graying hair and a wind-lined face. When he grimaced from pain, his lips stretched white.

"Can you sit?" Mush Jim asked. "Does your neck hurt?"

Without answering, the man sat down and leaned against the high seat. Fresh blood trickled from the wound. His face was gray.

"Get his boots off, Billie," Tiger said. He pressed one hand against the man's arm. "He's bleeding bad," he told Mush Jim. "Let the boys off at camp, and we'll run him over to the hospital." He tore off his own shirt and twisted it to make a tourniquet.

"It's just . . . a broken arm," the man gasped, grimacing again. "I don't . . . want no Indian . . . foolin' around with me."

Tiger remained stony-faced. He pulled the tourniquet tightly about the man's arm. "Rub his legs, boys. Keep the circulation going," he instructed, and the boys set to work.

Minutes later the airboat roared up to the bank and the boys piled out.

"Run, Billie," yelled Tiger. "Bring the *sofkee!*"

Billie tore up the path, the dog barking at his heels, skidded into the cookhouse, bumped into Grandmother, grabbed the pail of gruel and the big spoon, and raced back again to the airboat, his heart pounding.

"Drink," Tiger said, and put the *sofkee* spoon to the man's lips. The man sputtered and coughed. Tiger waited and gave him more. This time he drank.

"Now we will go," Tiger said, and adjusted the tourniquet again.

The man opened his eyes and tried to struggle. "Don't want no Indian," he gasped

"You're going to the hospital," Tiger said.

"My plane—"

"I'll see what I can salvage from the wreck," Mush Jim promised. "Hold on, now. Don't try to talk."

"No Indian . . . " the man said again, but the motor roared, and the airboat bolted off across the dark water.

Abraham sat on the wooden platform of his sleeping chickee, wrinkled face tilted up toward the night sky. Sihoki shuffled back and forth beside the fire, jabbing at the logs.

"Better the swamp should have him than Mush Jim should bring him here," she hissed, spitting through her teeth. "Next time he will be back to hunt and to fish."

Billie and Charlie lay down on their bedding and thought about the evening.

"How come he didn't want an Indian working on his arm?" Billie said at last. "If Father hadn't stopped the bleeding, he'd be dead."

"Aw, I don't know," Charlie answered. "He's probably half crazy. Out of his head. You get that way if you're hurt bad enough. No telling what a guy will say. He'll feel different tomorrow."

"I don't think he was out of his head," Billie said. "I think he meant it. Like Father was going to make it worse or something." He lay there thinking about all the times someone in the family had been hurt. Tiger had been doctor to them all for as long as he could remember. Only once had they gone to the clinic in town, and that was when Watsie had an eye infection. And sometimes they went to the dentist.

What would they have done if Tiger hadn't been around to take care of them? The pilot was luckier than he deserved.

"I'm going with Mush Jim tomorrow to strip the plane," Charlie said, letting down his canopy.

"I'll go too," said Billie.

He lay awake for some time, partly because he was waiting for his father and uncle to get back, and partly because he knew that Grandfather was still sitting out there in the night, talking to the trees and the stars, because he was a part of them. Finally, Billie lifted his canopy and went over to the chickee where old Abraham sat, bony knees crossed, as though he had fallen asleep sitting up.

"Grandfather," Billie whispered, sitting down beside him. "You asleep?"

"No. I am waiting for Mush Jim," Abraham answered.

Billie sat quietly for a while. It was time to be part of the forest, part of the earth—to talk to the wind and listen to it sing. The breeze rustled the palmetto thatch where it hung down low on the sides of the chickee. High above came the lone call of the brown and white limpkin, echoing out across the dark river of grass. Billie would sit here with Grandfather and keep him company till the men came back.

"Is it very hard to leave your clan, Grandfather?" he asked finally, still thinking of Tiger and the way he had become a part of Sihoki's camp. "Is it hard for a man to leave his own people?"

Abraham ignored the question. "Panther was my

clan," he said instead. "Out of the mountain we came and down to the water."

"Tell it to me again, Grandfather," urged Billie, knowing the old man wanted to talk.

Abraham opened his dark mouth once or twice before the words finally came.

"Long time ago, Indians were in the mountain. Like ten-month-old babies they slept in the mountain. Then Panther Clan and Wind Clan dug and dug until they were out. They were like brothers, for they came out together. Deer and Wolf Clans were also very close. Both have four feet. Then came Snake Clan and all the others, and Snake is called King. Panther followed Wind Clan from the navel of the earth. Panther Clan had a big head. It could not get out. Wind Clan came out like a whirlwind. Wind Clan came out on one side of the roots which grew on the mountain. Panther people came out on the other side. Bird Clan came out third, and Snake Clan last. Trees grew up fast so that Panther was held down. Wind Clan blew up the roots, and then Panther came out. They all came out like babies. And that is the way my people came on earth."

Even though Billie had heard this story many times, he waited until he was sure it was over. Sometimes Abraham forgot and repeated parts of it, but Billie didn't mind. When Abraham had been quiet for some time, however, Billie asked, "Did you ever miss your own people after you went to live with the Wind Clan?"

Abraham did not take his eyes off the sky. "I needed a wife," he said. "Sihoki was my wife."

It was as simple as that. Billie had heard his grandfather say it before: "I needed Sihoki." There is no word in the Mikasuki language for love. Instead, the people say, "I need you," but the feeling is the same.

It was very late when Mush Jim and Tiger came home. Even Grandfather had stopped waiting and fallen asleep in his chickee, and Billie had covered him up before he went back to his own bed. But Billie woke when he heard voices around the fire in the cookhouse, and he opened his eyes and listened.

"Don't waste your time," he heard Tiger say gruffly. "Let the plane rot."

Tiger wanted nothing more to do with it. But Mush Jim didn't like to make enemies. He had promised to see what he could salvage from the plane, so he felt he ought to do it. On Saturday morning he set out with Billie and Charlie. Tiger turned his back and hoed the garden instead.

The wings of the plane were slowly disappearing beneath the water. Soon the entire cabin would be flooded. The door hung open and Mush Jim checked for snakes before he crawled inside. Hacking away with his ax, he chopped out everything that would come loose. The right half of the fuselage was smashed and wrinkled like an accordion, but Mush Jim was able to bring out the radio and part of the instrument panel. Then, wrapping his legs in burlap, he climbed out and waded around to the motor. The saw grass was razor sharp.

The nose of the plane was already down in the

mud and the propellers were shattered. His muscles bulging beneath the sleeves of his tee shirt, Mush Jim hacked and grunted and tried to chop the motor away from its struts. For fifteen minutes mud flew, but the water kept closing in.

"It won't come," he said, and dropped his ax over the side of the boat, crawling in after it, wiping the mud from his face and sinking down to catch his breath. "Wedged in there so tight it won't budge, and probably no good now to anybody."

Suddenly, from somewhere behind them, came a deep, loud hiss, like wind blowing through a cave, and a long green snout rose up out of the swamp, the jaws open, spilling water out of its cavernous mouth like a river over the rocks. Rows of sharp teeth glistened on the top and bottom.

Billie gave a yell, stumbling backwards as an alligator's huge tail lashed at the water, spewing swamp muck over them.

"The Big One!" Charlie cried. "It must be, Mush Jim! Look!"

It was certainly the largest alligator Billie's uncle had ever seen. He couldn't believe the length of the tail. Again the alligator opened its mouth, and a deep windy hiss rushed out.

Mush Jim leaned over the side of the boat inspecting the monster. "He's a good fifteen feet!" he yelled. "Must be the one Fraser saw! Look at that tail!"

The open mouth was wide enough for a man's whole head and then some. Suddenly, without warning, the alligator charged the boat, turning as it came, and slapped against the side with its tail. The airboat reeled, rose slightly, and landed smacking against the water. Leaping forward, Mush Jim grabbed for the starting lever and got the engine going. Instantly the alligator submerged, only to rise on the other side and lash again from the other direction.

"Wow!" Charlie yelled, his eyes wide. "He's crazy for us, Mush Jim! Look at him!"

Mush Jim turned the engine on high. This time the Big One went under again and stayed, and a moment later the airboat was heading for camp.

On the school bus Monday, Billie told Jeffrey Miller about the Big One.

"Weren't you scared?" Jeff asked. "I'd be shaking all over the place."

"I was, when it hit the boat."

"Boy, you really have the excitement," Jeff said, staring glumly out the window. "Nothing like that ever happens to me. You know the most exciting thing I ever did?"

"What?"

"One time we went to Michigan to visit my grandmother at Christmas and I went down a long hill on a sled. That's all. Big deal!"

"I never saw snow," Billie told him to make him feel better.

"I never did either till then. I was real little and when we got there, there wasn't any. When we got up in the morning, there was. I just went outside and looked and looked, and you know what I said when I came back in? 'Mommy, I think there's something wrong with outdoors.' "

They both laughed.

"I've seen pictures of snowball fights," Billie said. "How do you make a snowball?"

"You just pick up a handful of snow like this." Jeffrey reached in his lunch sack and pulled out an orange. "Then you pack it down like this, and keep turning it around and around, and then . . ." He pulled back his arm. "You let it go—!"

Without warning, the orange flew from his hand and went straight for the driver as Jeff gasped. A moment later the orange hit the windshield, grazing the driver's ear, and split. Orange juice trickled down the window.

The driver gave a yell and pulled over on the side of the road.

"Hey, Miller, now you're in for it!" somebody yelled.

The driver stood up and came back.

"I didn't mean to," Jeff said honestly. "I really didn't! I was showing Billie how to make a snowball. It slipped. Honest!"

The driver looked at him skeptically. "Okay, show Billie how you're going to clean it up."

The other boys whistled and cheered as Jeffrey went up to the front of the bus and mopped the juice, grinning sheepishly. When he came back to his seat he said, "See? That's all that ever happens to me. Dumb things like that. Know what I'd like to do? Stay overnight with you sometime. Do you think I could?"

"Sure," Billie said, and then he thought about Sihoki. "I'll have to ask," he added. But it would be great having Jeff there. Charlie would like him too.

It was two weeks before the pilot came to get the instruments from his plane. Billie was sitting in Mush Jim's boat shack doing his homework when an Oldsmobile drove up and two men got out. One had his arm in a cast, and Billie recognized him right away.

They stood beside the car a moment, talking quietly to each other, and then came over.

"Hey, kid, your dad around?"

"He's at work," Billie answered.

"Who's the guy back there by the canal?" asked the tall man who had come with the pilot.

"Mush Jim—he's my uncle."

"Well, that's who we want to see."

Billie put down his pencil and came out of the shack. "Your arm better now?" he asked.

The pilot smiled a little. "It's coming along okay."

Billie went down to the canal in back where his uncle was replacing one of the boards on the dock.

"The pilot's here," he said.

Mush Jim looked up, wiped his arm across his eyes, and continued hammering. "Be up in a minute," he said.

Billie went back up the bank and around by the Oldsmobile.

"Probably going to charge you five times what they're worth," the tall man was saying to the other.

Billie stood silently with his hands in his pockets.

"If he does, he'll have a hard time collecting," the pilot answered. He noticed Billie and stopped.

"Mush Jim'll be up in a minute," Billie said sullenly. He didn't like what they said. Mush Jim had never cheated anybody.

Billie's uncle came up the bank and around the shack to the car.

"Afternoon," said the pilot, and smiled. "Guess you recognize me."

Mush Jim smiled back. "You look pretty good now."

"You guys did all right. I had a bad fracture and a broken rib, but I'm lucky I got out alive, I guess." He waited a moment and said, "I came for the parts to my plane. You said you'd try to get them out for me."

Mush Jim motioned toward the shack. "They're inside."

The radio and pieces of the instrument panel were piled in one corner. "That's all I could bring out," he told them. "The nose was in the mud. By now the wings are probably under."

The tall man looked at the pilot and then at Mush Jim. He gave a short laugh and scratched one ear. "Hard to believe you'd go to all that trouble and leave the motor behind."

"Too hard to get at," Mush Jim said. "Not worth it."

The tall man stopped smiling and shifted his weight to one leg, arms folded across his chest. "Now look, chief, I happen to know that a guy doesn't leave a good motor behind. What do you plan to do with it—sell it yourself?"

Billie couldn't believe what they were saying. His face grew hot, and his eyes narrow with anger. He looked up at his uncle. He could tell by the way his jaw flinched that Mush Jim was angry too.

"This is all I could do," Mush Jim said, his mouth rigid, and Billie had never seen him like that before.

"Look, I'm grateful to you for getting me out," the pilot said, and he seemed embarrassed. "If there's ever anything I can do, well . . . I'm grateful. I really am. But you said you'd try for that motor, and the water's not all that deep."

But the tall man swore and stepped forward. "It's no favor to pull a man out alive and then rob him," he said tersely. "I wasn't born yesterday. Stealing's a crime whether a plane's sitting right here or out in the glades. Now you better make up your mind to tell us where that motor's at."

Billie could take it no longer.

"Why don't you just get out of here?" he cried, and his voice broke. "Mush Jim doesn't want your old engine! He didn't have to go out there and get anything at all! He didn't have to rescue anybody, either!"

"Billie!" Mush Jim turned on him, frowning, and instantly Billie stopped, breathing hard. He dug his fingernails into the palms of his hands and stared at the ground.

"Do you want to see your plane?" Mush Jim said to the pilot. "Come on and I'll take you. You can get the motor out yourself."

The tall man shrugged. "Hell, I'm not going out there in that boat with him," he muttered. "Slit your throat soon as your back was turned."

"Hank, shut up," said the pilot. He turned to Mush Jim. "Look, I believe you. If you couldn't get the motor out, then I couldn't either. The plane was a mess. I know that."

Mush Jim didn't answer.

"How much do I owe you for getting the radio and instrument panel?" asked the pilot, pulling out his wallet.

"Nothing."

The man stared. "Oh, come on. You took me to the hospital . . . stopped the bleeding . . . saved my life." He handed Mush Jim a twenty-dollar bill.

"Take the parts," said Mush Jim, without moving.

The pilot looked uncomfortable. He turned to Billie. "Here, kid, you take it for him."

Billie remained motionless, hands in his pockets, eyes blazing and his cheeks as well.

The pilot turned away. He picked up some of the parts with one hand, and the tall man got the rest. They dumped them in the back of the car and got in, the tall man driving. The Oldsmobile backed out of the parking lot, paused a moment on the highway, and then roared off. Soon the car was out of sight. Still Mush Jim didn't move.

Billie uneasily dug his toe into the dirt, making a little row of deep gouges.

"Billie," said his uncle, "that wasn't the way."

Billie pressed his lips together. "They made me mad," he mumbled. "I wanted to—to kill them. Especially the big guy."

"And the hate would go on," said Mush Jim. "If

48

a man wants to be a snake, you don't have to keep him company."

He went down to the dock and began hammering again. Billie walked back to the little table where his school books lay. Then what was the Indian way? Just stand there like Mush Jim, hating but not speaking it? To have nothing more to do with them, as Tiger was doing? What was so wrong with sounding off? He hadn't said half of what he might. He hadn't even told the men about the alligator. Mush Jim could have been killed trying to get the dumb engine out. He began to wish they'd left the pilot there and that the Big One had come along and eaten him slowly, beginning at the toes.

He looked down and saw the twenty-dollar bill lying on the table beside his school books. He stared at it a moment, as though it were too dirty to touch, and then took it down to his uncle.

"They left this on the table," he said.

Mush Jim went on hammering. "Give it to Grandmother," he said, without missing a stroke. "I'd only spend it for gin."

Four

WHEN Billie gave his grandmother the money, she stuffed it in the neck of her blouse without a word. She saw no reason why they should not accept it. Mush Jim had earned it—every cent.

"What would you have said to those men, Grandfather?" Billie asked when he'd told Abraham the story. He squatted down beside the old man who was busily scraping a new batch of boiled garfish, and the glistening heap of scales grew higher and higher.

"The same as Mush Jim told them, Billie." Abraham paused and pressed his gums together once or twice. "But I would not let them make me angry."

Billie rocked back on his heels and plunked down on the grass. "You mean you'd just stand there?"

"No. If they did not believe me, I would go back to my work, so my eyes would not look upon them longer."

Grandfather was hopeless. He was even worse than Mush Jim!

"But wouldn't you even *feel* mad?"

The old man put down the fish he was holding and brushed off the scales that clung to his brown hands. "Why should I be an angry one, Billie? If a pig steps on your foot, you do not get angry and bite unless you also are a pig. Then you would make much noise. But a man, he just walks away. An Indian is such a man."

"Just walk away!" Billie said. "I couldn't do that, Grandfather! I just couldn't. It would seem like giving in."

Abraham's eyes glittered. "Never, Billie. We are Mikasuki. If someone steals from me, if he attacks me, if he hurts those who are part of me, then I fight. And how I fight! But if he is not wise in the mouth, if he shows his ignorance by saying foolish things, then I lift my head above him and turn my feet in another direction so that my ears can listen to the birds and the water instead of stupid talk. That is the Indian way. We are proud because we are of the earth, of the trees, of the rivers, and of the stars."

Grandfather was indeed more Indian than Billie ever dreamed of becoming.

"I'll never make it," Billie murmured.

"Make it?"

"The sky path—to the city in the sky. I'll get lost first thing."

"I did not say it was easy," said Grandfather.

As the family ate from the big pot that evening, Billie remembered about Jeffrey Miller.

"Mother," he said, and he realized that he was about to ask a question he had never asked before in his life. "Could Jeff Miller stay here some night? He could come home from school with me and go back again the next morning."

Alice Tommie stared at him across the fire. "You would bring the boy here?" The rattle of spoons had stopped, and everyone looked at Billie.

"To *sleep?*" Alice asked again, incredulously.

"Couldn't very well ask him to sit up all night," Mush Jim joked, wiping his plate clean with a piece of fried bread. But nobody smiled.

Sihoki made a squealing sound in her throat. "Ei! What is this, then? A bus station, that strangers should come here and sleep?"

"He's no stranger, Grandmother," Billie said. "He's my best friend at school. And Mush Jim knows his dad."

"He's the man who buys the frog legs from the boys, Mother," Mush Jim said. "A good man. He's not a trader, really. But he goes to Miami every Friday on business, so he stops at some of the Indian camps and takes their frogs to the restaurants on the coast. Keeps only a small part of the earnings for himself.

He's also a volunteer for the Wildlife Federation. I've known him for three years. Billie and Jeff get along fine together."

The camp was so quiet that Billie knew now why he'd never even considered asking before.

"No one but our own people have been to this place," Alice Tommie said, and her voice was firm. "If we lived anywhere else, then . . ."

The eating resumed, more quietly than before. But Mush Jim continued.

"Can't hardly expect Billie to go to school and not take on new ways," he commented. But no one answered, and Billie knew it was useless to keep on. Sihoki would never hear of it.

The night air was hot, and neither Billie nor Charlie felt like sleeping. Charlie got down the Chinese checkers, and the two boys lay on their stomachs in the chickee, clunking the marbles around over the top of the metal board.

"Hey, you missed a great move, Billie," Charlie said. "Take your turn over and start here." It was a fantastic jump, and Billie's marble landed in the farthest hole of Charlie's triangle. He looked around the board to find a good move for Charlie in return, but Charlie had already found one. Charlie was by far the better player. When he moved a marble in a certain way, however, Billie said it couldn't be done.

"Check the rules," Billie said, but his brother handed the paper to him. It was hard to remember that Charlie couldn't read. It wasn't fair that a guy so smart in his head couldn't even read letters on paper.

Billie was still thinking about it when he went to school the next day.

Jeff Miller didn't say anything more about coming to Billie's camp, and Billie was glad. It would have been hard to say no, especially since he and Jeff and Charlie could have such a good time together.

The class was studying Florida's history. For several weeks they had worked on a map of the state which covered half the blackboard. They had memorized a list of its great men and women and even written the governor for a picture of himself to pin on the bulletin board. Mrs. Kelly told them that she herself was a Floridian by birth, and her ancestors, too, had played a part in Florida's past.

Each day the students were given library time to work on a paper about a major event in Florida's history, something, Mrs. Kelly said, that interested them particularly. Jeff Miller was writing about the first railroad built to Key West and how a hurricane swept it out to sea in 1935. But Billie was writing about what he knew best—the stories Grandfather had told him about the Seminole Wars and the great Indian leader, Osceola.

There were times when Billie lay on his back in the chickee, listening to the flute song of the whip-poorwill, that the air seemed heavy with spirits of the braves. Who knew how many had stood on this very ground defying the white man to come and take them away to the strange land beyond the Mississippi?

As far back as Billie could remember, when the family bundled up against the chill of January and huddled around the fire, old Abraham talked of Osceola and the men who fought with him. One of the men was Abraham's own grandfather, and Abraham told the story as his grandfather had told it to him. It was as though Osceola himself were there in the chickee, his glossy black hair falling about his face, two long feathers drooping from the cloth turban around his head.

The story Billie liked best was about a General named Thompson who called the Indian chiefs together and angrily demanded that they sign a treaty which would send all their people to the west. Osceola had stepped forward, eyes flashing, drawn his knife, and pinned the treaty paper to the table, saying loudly, "This land is ours. This is the way I will sign all such treaties." And when Abraham said these words, the flesh on Billie's arms and legs turned to goose bumps, and the wind in the cypress sounded like the very breath from Osceola's lungs.

Billie knew how the story ended, for he had heard again and again how Osceola vowed that any chief who agreed to move his people west on command of the white soldiers should be killed. The government said that if the Indians would not give up their homes peacefully and move, they would be moved by force. Osceola and a band of fifty warriors attacked Fort King. General Thompson and several others were killed.

Now Osceola was the real leader of the Seminoles,

and in 1836 he sent a letter of defiance to still another general who had been sent to fight him. Abraham knew the letter by heart. With his eyes half closed and his face tilted upward, voice quavery, he would recite the words that his grandfather had told him: "You have guns, so have we. You have powder and lead and so have we. Your men will fight, and so will ours—till the last drop of Seminole blood has moistened the dust of his hunting ground!"

And so, Billie wrote in his paper, the fighting had gone on between the government of Andrew Jackson and the Seminoles. The Indians fled deeper and deeper into the Everglades, hiding their children in holes in the ground so that the soldiers could not find them. But Osceola was finally captured, and died in prison. Other men rose up to lead the people: Alligator, Wild Cat, Sam Jones, and Billy Bowlegs. Again and again the Indians were tricked. Even bloodhounds were used to chase them out of hiding.

Finally in 1858, the Seminole Wars ended. Many Indians had given up and gone west. But not all. Not Abraham's grandfather. He and a few hundred Mikasuki remained in the Everglades where they could not be found, refusing to surrender, ready to flee at a moment's notice. And it was there that Billie's great-great-grandfather lived out his life in the forests he loved so well—where the howl of the wolf and the scream of the panther made his music, and his children grew tall and straight as the corn in his garden. All this Billie told about in his paper.

It was Billie's job to wash the blackboards on

Thursdays. While the other children were outside at recess, he got a bucket from the janitor's closet, filled it with water, and ran his sponge over the slate, making it dark black, ready for the afternoon's arithmetic. Jeffrey Miller did the blackboards on Fridays, and sometimes they wrote silly messages to each other in the corner of the far blackboard under the calendar which the other children skipped.

In case of fire, stand outside and clap, Jeff had written once, and the following week Billie scribbled, *Don't just stand there watching it burn. Toss in a couple books.*

Mrs. Kelly was checking spelling papers at her desk, and her red pencil moved quickly, jerkily, down each column, flashing a quick mark here and there and scribbling a grade at the top.

For a while there was no sound in the room but the swish of the wet sponge and the slight whir of the electric clock on the wall. Billie was thinking about clocks as he worked. He had been eight years old when his father enrolled him in the first grade, and had learned so fast that each year he was promoted up two grades. On opening day, when he entered first grade with all the little kids, the clock on the wall was the only one he had ever seen. He didn't even know what it was. There was nothing he could see that was so special about it, and yet the teacher seemed to watch it anxiously all day long.

"Time to clean up now," she would say just when everybody was having a marvelous time painting horses. Or, "We've got only two minutes left," when they were well started with the rhythm instruments and always, it seemed, when Billie had the cymbals. Billie could not understand it, how a silly round thing on the wall could tell a grown lady what to do.

"Why don't you just throw a rock at it?" he had asked his teacher, and she had laughed.

"But I want to follow the clock," she had explained. "That's the only way we'd get everything done."

Billie couldn't understand it then, and sometimes he didn't even understand it now. His father and uncle never looked at a clock, and yet they seemed to get everything done. When the shadows in the camp were a certain length or the birds sounded a certain way or an owl hooted or the alligators' eyes at the edge of the lagoon took on a certain gleam, it was time for certain things. The Seminoles ate when they were hungry and slept when they were tired. But the teachers at school obeyed their little round watches whether they felt like it or not. What a crazy way to live.

"Billie."

It wasn't the first-grade teacher now, but Mrs. Kelly who was talking to him. He stopped and turned around.

"That was a good paper you wrote on the Seminole Wars, as far as it went."

Now what did she mean by that? Was this a compliment? Billie didn't answer. He fumbled awkardly with the sponge for a moment and then continued rubbing the slate.

"You wrote some things I'd never heard before—

58

little details—almost as though you had really been there. You have a great imagination."

It was no compliment, Billie decided.

"I didn't just make it up," he said softly. "It's the way my grandfather told it to me. And the way it was told to him. The way it really happened."

The red pencil in Mrs. Kelly's hand kept right on clicking. "Well, it reads nicely, but I had hoped you would do your research in the library."

"I did go to the library," Billie told her, "but the books didn't tell the way the Indians thought about it." He was aware of the defiance in his voice—ever so slight.

The teacher noticed it too, because she put her pencil down and cleared her throat a little. "But there's another side to the story, you know. The Indians weren't all saints."

Billie didn't know what a saint was. "It was Indian land," he said, and his voice was low. "Everyplace the Indians were, the government wanted them someplace else. And everyplace the government sent them was worse than the place before. All the Indians wanted were their homes and the land that the generals were trying to take away from them." Maybe because he was scrubbing the blackboard as he talked instead of looking at her, it came easier. He had never imagined he could say what he did.

"When you're a soldier, you have to do what you're ordered," said Mrs. Kelly. "The President had ordered the generals to round up the Indians and send them west to live with the others. The generals had to do it. It was their job, whether or not one agrees with it. They didn't want to fight. They would have preferred that not a single life would be lost, but the Indians resisted." She was talking faster now, earnestly, as though she just had to convince him. "There were terrible atrocities on both sides. Horrible things happened, not only to soldiers but to women and children as well. I can understand how the Seminoles would feel, but the government soldiers were people, too. They also had wives and children, and you didn't put any of their feelings in your report." And suddenly she added, "General Thompson was the cousin of my great grandmother."

Billie's arms moved slowly down the blackboard. He had to say it. Now! Open his mouth, let the words come out. Say it! Now! "It was my great-great grandfather who fought with Osceola," he said, and his heart pounded so hard he felt it would leap out of his chest.

The silence in the room was suffocating. The possibility came to both of them at once that maybe Billie's great-great grandfather himself had killed General Thompson.

"I see," said Mrs. Kelly. Then she smiled and said quickly, almost embarrassed, "Well, we don't have to go on being enemies, do we?"

Billie smiled a little too. "No," he said. Of course Mrs. Kelly wasn't his enemy. But she wasn't exactly a friend, either.

Sundays were good days in the camp. They would

60

have been even better if Mush Jim were home, but lots of people came for airboat rides on the weekends, so he stayed at the canal waiting for tourists. Around the camp, things were slow and lazy and quiet. Even the dog seemed to know that it was Sunday. He would rise, stretch himself long with his hind legs straight out behind him, his back sagging, and yawn widely. Then he would snap his jaws suddenly as the yawn was over and wag his tail, ready for breakfast and whatever the day would bring.

Sunday was no different for Alice Tommie and Sihoki, however. They sat cross-legged on the floor of Grandmother's chickee, weaving sweet grass baskets or cranking the handle of their hand-operated sewing machine. Rapidly they fed the shirts and blouses through as row after row of bright designs were stitched on each garment. They sang or talked as they worked. Watsie, climbing in and out of her low hammock, leaned against them watching the work, begging for a song or stretching her hand out to the dog and pulling it back again when he licked her fingers.

Early on Sunday mornings, Tiger and Abraham would go out in the dugout canoe to fish where the waters were quiet. It was the same canoe that Abraham had made twenty years before, and one of the few left in the Everglades now that the Indians owned airboats. Abraham had carved it from the trunk of a cypress tree, chosen with care, aged in water, and skillfully chiseled out with an adz.

When the fish were in, Tiger would take his hoe

and go to the garden to cultivate the corn and green beans. Watsie would follow along behind and sometimes pick up the clods of dirt that rolled from Tiger's hoe.

There was something about this September Sunday, however, that wasn't quite the same. The dog was restless. He stayed close to Tiger and sometimes lifted his nose and sniffed the air.

"He acts as though the Big One's around," said Charlie, as he and Billie tossed a volley ball over a string which they had tied between two trees.

But Tiger seemed to sense something too. Every so often he stopped with his hand on his hoe and looked out over the water, turning his head slowly, looking in all directions. Then he would go on with his work, saying nothing.

About noon, Tiger got into the canoe and paddled out into the lagoon, turning eastward toward the big stretch of saw grass.

He was gone only a short time. The dog heard him coming back and dàshed to meet him. Tiger came striding up the path from the water and went at once to the chickee where Mother and Grandmother were sewing.

"The saw grass pollen is heavy in the air," he said, and the family knew at once what that meant.

Five

A HURRICANE was churning somewhere in the
Atlantic. The Tommie family had neither newspaper
nor radio, but they always knew when a big storm
was on the way.

People often wondered how the Indians knew.
Some said that the Seminoles were magic. Some said
that when the bloom was on the saw grass, it meant a
hurricane was coming. But the saw grass bloomed at
certain times whether there was a hurricane or not.
The truth was that an atmospheric calm made the
saw grass pollen visible for several days before a
hurricane moved inland. When the Indians saw the

pollen floating in the air, they knew it was time to move their children and possessions to higher ground.

It was no cause for panic, however. Only two years before, the Tommie family had gone to the school to wait out a storm, and when it was over, only the cookhouse had lost its roof. So when Tiger told Alice and Sihoki the news, they finished the garments they were working on before packing up to leave.

Some of the things would stay behind in camp—the heavier kettles, the pigs and chickens—and some things would be taken to Mush Jim's boat shack, which stood on higher ground. The family would carry some of their clothes and bedding on their backs when they went to the school, where people from low-lying homes all around came for protection.

The dog knew that something was different now. He trailed close behind Billie and Charlie, ears laid back, whining as the boys stuffed clothes and blankets into the big cloth sacks that served as suitcases.

Abraham was always silent when they left camp, even if it were only a visit to the Big Cypress reservation or perhaps one of the stores along the Trail. He did not enjoy a trip to the highway where cars whizzed and the neon lights of gas stations blinked and the tourists followed him about with their cameras because he still wore the long shirt of the traditional Seminole men. He did not care at all for the alligators in pens or the souvenir shops or the gravel parking lots which hurt his feet. A trip away from camp was merely something to be endured, and he and Sihoki drew into themselves, sitting off silently together with half-closed eyes, nourished by the inner quiet which they took with them, as though the pumpkins and tomatoes, the fox and the panther, had somehow come along.

Watsie was upset by the sudden bustle, so Grandmother put her back into her hammock and rocked it with one hand as she sang:

Swing, Jonny-Willie, in your pretty red hammock,
    Frog in swamp make glad night song;
Alligator bay down in Big Cypress,
    Hammock hide Jonny when bear trot along.

Dark come quick when sun go down
    Wind make music in tall pine tree;
Hammock swing out and hammock swing in,
    But sleep catch Jonny, he no can see.

Screech owl laugh and wildcat snarl,
    Bat swoop low, but Jonny no afraid,
Big Chief tell: No harm can come
    To Seminole baby in deep Everglade.

Swing, Jonny-Willie, in your pretty red hammock,
    Mockingbird call come low and sweet;
Stars make crown for your moss pillow,
    Moonbeam gild your little brown feet.*

By the time the song was finished, Watsie was almost asleep. She lay very still, her eyelids drooping, and the dog lay down on his belly in the dust.

*From THE SEMINOLES: DWELLERS OF THE EVERGLADES by William C. Emerson. © 1954 by William C. Emerson. Reprinted by permission of the publishers, Exposition Press, Inc.

As the afternoon shadows lengthened, the saw grass rippled in waves like a field of wheat. The clouds moved as a river in one direction against a gray sky. Tiger set out with a load in the dugout canoe, and when he came back, Mush Jim was ahead of him in the airboat.

The winds were whipping in sudden long gusts that made the younger trees toss their branches wildly.

"I hear that the storm's shifting," Mush Jim told them, tying up the boat. "Hurricane's heading directly in, and picking up speed. Be here tomorrow, probably."

As the sky grew darker, the wind grew stronger, banging the few remaining pots together and lashing at the palmetto thatching above. If ever the great Osceola seemed to be present in the camp, it was now. All through the evening meal the wind shrieked around the posts and whistled through the rafters. The dog howled in mournful anticipation, and the pigs ran squealing through the underbrush, taking refuge under the floor of the chickees.

Darkness engulfed the camp early, and the family sat closely around the fire. Billie imagined for a moment that it was a hundred and fifty years ago and that he and his family were hiding out here on the island, listening for the ominous splash of a paddle or thud of a boot. He shivered and Sihoki put one fat arm around him, but it wasn't the cold that made him shake.

The wind increased steadily during the night. The

family slept together in one chickee, each up against the others for warmth. Billie slept fitfully, and was glad when the morning light broke through the forest. There would be no work today or school either. All morning Tiger, Mush Jim, Billie, and Charlie worked to tie down the cooking pots, hoist the other possessions to the rafters, and secure the canoe to the trunk of a cypress tree on the bank. Then they rode the airboat to Mush Jim's shack where they tied it down, and took the pickup truck to the school.

Mrs. Sykes, wife of the Methodist minister, was there with cocoa for the children. The Red Cross truck arrived at five with coffee and sandwiches, and as the large basement room began to fill up, families staked out little areas on the floor where they spread their blankets and tried to get fussy children to nap.

The wind rose to fifty miles an hour with sixty-mile gusts. Billie and Charlie stayed at the front door where the men stood in groups talking, looking down on the road below. Debris was everywhere— branches, dry palm fronds, and Spanish moss. Big cypress trees swayed their heads, and creatures of the swamp found refuge wherever they could.

And then the rain came—torrents of rain, pouring in sheets and buckets against the windows. The moan of the wind grew louder and higher, swooping down upon them at times like a freight train.

Time passed slowly. Tiger and Mush Jim sat speculating about the damage that was being done to the chickees. Abraham squatted in one corner of the all-purpose room and ate the food that Sihoki had brought along, the dog close beside him, ears laid back, unused to the noise of so many people all together. Billie picked up Watsie and took her to a window to see the mother possum and her young taking refuge on the ledge. Then Watsie discovered the drinking fountain in the hallway and amused herself by squirting the water on and off.

Outside it was raining sideways, not drops, but long streaks of glistening water. Some Indians didn't seek shelter at all. Some, who raised cattle on the nearby Brighton reservation, preferred to stay with the animals right through the storm, and enjoyed their reputation for being able to quiet the herds in a hurricane.

Mrs. Sykes brought in some toys from the kindergarten room for the youngsters, and sent Billie and Charlie to bring down an armload of books from the library for the older children.

It was the room that Billie loved best—a soft room, with a rug on the floor and a blue rocking chair with a pillow on it. There were loads of pictures on the walls and shelves and tables covered with books. Baseball stories lined one shelf, mystery books another. There were animal stories, ghost stories, books about great men and women, fairy tales, and almost any other story Billie could imagine.

It was Charlie's first time in the library. He stepped cautiously on the rug, as though it were someone's blanket, and stared for a moment at the blue rocker.

"That's the reading chair," Billie explained. "Everybody tries to get it first. We have to take turns."

Slowly Charlie moved down the row of animal books, pulled one out, and stared at the cover. It was a book about training horses, and there was a picture of a pinto pony on front. Charlie was fascinated.

"What's it about?" he asked.

"Training horses," Billie told him, "for shows and circuses and stuff. Bring it along, and I'll read it to you when we get downstairs."

But Charlie put the book back, and Billie knew at once why. Charlie wouldn't have wanted anyone to see Billie reading to him. He didn't want the others to know that he didn't go to school.

"Charlie," Billie said quickly, not wanting to lose the chance. "You could learn to read if you had somebody good to teach you. There's a special class at school for older kids like you who need more help. You could go to school with me and start out slow. Why, I'll bet you'd be ahead of me before you hardly knew it."

"I can't, Billie. I just can't." It was the first time Charlie had said it.

"But why?"

"It's not just the learning. It's not just being in with kids who are smaller than me. It's . . . it's just . . . I wasn't made for sitting in a chair all day and holding a pencil. Maybe, if I'd started when I was eight, like you . . . . But now I've got to feel the wind on my face and the sun on my back. I guess maybe there ought to be a school that meets outdoors just for people like me." He smiled his half smile that Billie knew so well and shrugged his shoulders. "Dumb Charlie, that's me," he said, and tried to grin, but he couldn't.

"You're *not* dumb!" Billie said fiercely. "Don't you ever say it. Mush Jim says if you even just joke about it, you'll have other people believing it too."

"Okay," said Charlie. "Happy Charlie, then."

But he wasn't. Billie knew. There were too many times Charlie needed to read and write, and was embarrassed because he couldn't.

At seven that evening, the power lines broke down, and there was no light in the school except the kerosene lamps which some of the refugees had brought with them. The full fury of the storm was upon them, and Mrs. Sykes herded everyone to the center hallway, away from the windows, where they were bedded down along the walls on blankets and sleeping bags. There were long rows of men, women, and children—Indians and whites, young and old, farmers from low-lying fields and tourists fleeing from Miami. Anyone who needed a refuge found it here.

Windows on the side away from the storm were left open an inch so that the tremendous pressure of the wind outside would not break them. Billie lay beside Charlie, staring up into darkness, listening to the storm that seemed to hurl itself against the school like some monstrous ocean animal. The dog trembled. Billie thought of the chickens and pigs that had been left back at camp and hoped they had found shelter somewhere inside the thick forest.

A window shattered in the all-purpose room and

then another. "It's all right," came the calm voice of Mrs. Sykes, sitting watch over the little groups in the hallway. "The Lord has you all in the palm of his hand."

A strange way to talk about the Great Spirit, Billie thought—the Great One who lived in the sky and never visited the earth.

It was daylight before the winds began to die down. As morning crept into the hallway, people woke and stirred, anxious to get back to their homes and see what damage had been done. Doors were thrown open, and the drops of water off drenched leaves came in a steady pat-patting sound, but the worst was over. Battered swamp birds preened their feathers. Schools, the radio said, would be closed for two days so that power lines could be repaired and the roads cleared.

Grandfather was never so happy as when he was going home. Tiger's pickup truck, which had been parked in the shelter of the school building, was unharmed except for a dent in the roof where a branch had fallen. As they made their way back along the road in the truck—the three men inside the cab and the women and children in back—they could see the walls of filling stations which had caved in, trees over the road, palm fronds, boxes, and boards in scattered profusion everywhere.

But Abraham could only smile. Nothing was so sweet as the thought of the mangrove swamp. Spending the night shut up in a box only convinced him all the more that man belonged outside and not in a cage.

He yearned for the fragrance of the mangos and papayas, for the place where the pigs ran wild in the swamp and the chickens scratched for food on the quiet bank of the lagoon.

And Billie, too, felt good about going home. He, too, longed to get back to the peace of the swamp.

It took almost an hour to reach Mush Jim's shack. Palms and cypress leaned at grotesque angles. Mountains of Spanish moss had been blown from the trees. Some parts of the road were impassable, and the family had to back up and go another way or get out and move the debris themselves. When they got to the boat shanty, they found that one side had caved in and the roof had blown away. The extra clothes and bedding lay strewn about the muddy ground. Skirts and jackets caught on twigs and branches like laundry out to dry. Like a plastic toy, the airboat had been turned upside down, despite its moorings, but miraculously had not been damaged.

Mush Jim stood with his hands in his pockets, surveying the mess.

"The wind was no brother to us this time," said Abraham quietly.

Without speaking, Tiger and Mush Jim righted the airboat and cleaned out the mud from the bottom. Then they all set out for camp in silence, Sihoki clicking her teeth all the way, and the dog standing up front, his tail wagging violently.

Somehow Billie knew even before they got there. Perhaps it was the oath Mush Jim muttered as they neared the island that told him, or the sudden way the dog whined. Maybe somehow the trees looked different, even from this far away. But he knew that something had happened, and when they reached the island, they saw that the camp was gone.

It did not even look like the same island. The water had risen so high that most of the ground was covered. There was no bank at all where Mush Jim had always docked before. This time the airboat drifted right in over the place where the cookhouse had stood and came to rest against one of the wooden posts that had held up the roof. The only thing remaining was the dugout canoe, still lashed to a tree. The chickees were gone. The roofs and the platforms were gone. Only a few posts remained, half buried in the water. One pig sat forlornly on a floating log, and the carcasses of several chickens floated by.

Strange noises came from Sihoki's throat as her old eyes took in the sight before her, as though she were in pain. And when Billie turned to speak to his grandfather, he saw tears in the old man's eyes and on his wrinkled cheeks. Abraham's lips moved, but he said nothing.

"It is gone." Alice Tommie was the first to speak, and she said all there was to say. The water would go down in time, but the family would have to find a new home.

They returned to Mush Jim's shack. They could build a new roof by evening, clean out the inside, and put the one wall back. At least it would be a place to sleep. Tomorrow, perhaps, Tiger and Mush Jim would go searching for a new island. They could not decide on it now.

They took the pig back with them. Mush Jim and Tiger were working on the roof of the shack when a second pickup truck turned in off the road and Mr. Miller got out. His mustache and beard showed up light brown against his yellow shirt. There was a sack of groceries in his arms.

"Thought you might need these," he said, and without waiting for thanks, asked, "What's the news? How's the camp?"

"Gone. Under water." Mush Jim came over and shook his hand.

"A dirty shame!" Jeff's father hunched his shoulders and stood with his eyes down, shaking his head. "Worst storm in five years. Big Cypress is under water, too, I hear. And it did a heck of a lot of damage south a ways. I got a couple windows broken, but that's all. I was lucky." He looked around. "You staying the night here?"

Mush Jim nodded. "We'll have the roof on and the floor cleaned out. It'll do till we find another camp. Thanks for the groceries, Ed."

"You'd do the same for me." Mr. Miller turned to go, then stopped suddenly and looked at Billie. "Hey, be okay if I took Billie home with me for a couple days? You haven't got much room here, and Jeff would love it. Be a break for the kids till school opens again."

"Can I?" Billie asked eagerly, hardly even thinking.

It took Tiger by surprise. Neither Sihoki nor Alice

had understood what the man asked, so Tiger had to answer. He looked over the wreckage of the shack and the little patch of muddy floor where the whole family was to sleep that night, and it seemed the most sensible thing to do. He nodded, and before he had time to explain it to Grandmother, Billie bounded for the truck.

It wasn't Jeffrey's house that was so strange, exactly. Billie had been in homes before. Some of his relatives on Big Cypress lived in houses with faucets in the bathrooms and switches that turned on the lights and soft and hard furniture for sitting. But something was very different about being here in Jeff's, and as soon as the screen door closed behind him, he knew.

On Big Cypress, in Seminole houses, the doors and windows were wide open all day and night, except when it was cold. Dogs and chickens wandered in and out just as they wandered in and out of a chickee.

But here, in Jeff's house, what was outside was kept that way, and what was in was in. There were screens on all the windows and screen doors as well. There was furniture for inside the house and special furniture that sat on the lawn. There were little gold-fish swimming around in a glass bowl inside the house and a big dog that had to stay out. Everything that couldn't come in was neatly lined up along the outside of the house, and before Jeffrey's little brother came in, he had to park his tricycle at the door and wipe his shoes.

Jeff didn't know that Billie was coming. He didn't even know that Billie was there till he walked in the room with the morning comics, stared at Billie like a creature from another planet, and threw the newspaper into the air.

"Yahoo!" he shrieked, and Mrs. Miller said, "Jeff! Use your *inside* voice!"

Oh, no! thought Billie. Inside and outside voices too!

"Thought you'd like company for a day or two," Mr. Miller grinned, as Jeff bounded over and pounded Billie on the back.

"Did the camp blow down?" Jeff asked, suddenly remembering the storm.

"It washed away," Billie told him. "Nothing's left. We've got to build someplace else."

"Oh, that's terrible!" said Jeff's mother, sitting down on the arm of the couch. "It was an awful storm. Ruined miles of the Miami beachfront. But we're glad you're here, Billie. This is Keith, Jeff's brother. You've heard about him, I suppose."

"I'm five!" Keith chirped.

"Five and ornery," said Jeff, grinning. "Come on, Billie, I'll show you around."

There were bunkbeds in Jeff's room, and other rooms just for washing or cooking or sleeping— like a lot of chickees built under the same roof.

The boys spent the afternoon shooting baskets on the driveway. Keith stood on the grass and ran after the ball if it rolled toward the street. Billie could hardly get used to the noise. All up and down the block, children were playing on the damp sidewalks—riding bikes and pulling wagons and skating. And everybody seemed to be shrieking all at once. It was ear-splitting, just like the playground at school.

There were hamburgers for supper, which Billie loved, and lemonade and potato salad. And lots of talk. Everybody talked, and it seemed as though they all began at once. They asked him questions when his mouth was full, and hardly let him answer before they asked him another. Keith asked if he had a pony and whether he could shoot a bow and arrow, and was disappointed when Billie said no.

"Hey, let the kid eat!" Mr. Miller laughed, so Keith made silly talk the rest of the meal, and Billie was glad to be left alone.

There was television after dinner and a couple games of Battleship. Then Mrs. Miller sent them to bed, and after fooling around in the bathroom and spraying each other with the shower nozzle, they went to bed, Jeff on the top bunk and Billie on the bottom.

"Hey, Billie," Jeff called from above. "You think I'll ever get to come to your camp?"

"Don't have any camp," said Billie. " 'Less you want to sleep in the mud."

"I mean, when you build another one."

"I don't know," Billie answered truthfully. "My mother—and my grandmother—they sort of don't like to have strangers around." He wished Jeff hadn't asked.

"Heck, I'm no stranger."

"You are to them, I guess."

Jeff thought it over. "Maybe I could just slip in sometime, you know, so I won't be strange any more. Then maybe they'll let me. Just tell me your address when you get moved, and I'll row out sometime."

"We never had an address."

"What? How do you get your mail, then?"

"Never get mail."

"You're pulling my leg."

"No, I'm not. I never got a letter in my life."

"I'll write you one, then, and the post office will have to find you."

"What'll you say in it?"

"I'll say . . . uh . . . 'Dear Billie, by the time you get this letter I'll be standing at your front door, 'cause I'm following the mailman there.' How's that?"

Billie laughed. "Don't have any front door."

"I give up," said Jeff. "I'll drop you a letter by helicopter."

"You fellas better get some sleep in there," came Mr. Miller's voice from the next room. "Almost eleven-thirty."

"Night, meathead," said Jeff, and Billie lay in the darkness grinning.

As the house grew still, however, Billie couldn't sleep. There were no animal cries, no birds, no sound of frogs splashing in the water, no alligator bellows. There came instead the roar of trucks from the highway a mile off, and it sounded like thunder on the roof. A neighbor's dog kept up a steady yipping that no one seemed to notice. Jeff's brother called for a drink and someone got up and went back to bed again. The house was quiet, but the trucks droned on.

It was hard to sleep here somehow. The house seemed too strange. Of course, it would seem strange crowded together in the boat shack too, but at least there would be the familiar sound of Sihoki's teeth clicking away in the darkness, the snoring grunts of Grandfather, and the scurryings of night animals in the brush.

Billie wondered if he should have come. He thought about the mess back at Mush Jim's. He had left without thinking of Charlie, without so much as a wave to Grandfather. He thought of the old man, as he'd seen him that morning in camp, with tears on his cheeks. Billie wished he had stayed with them to help out. If nothing else, he could have sat beside Grandfather as darkness fell to keep him from being so lonely.

He decided to go back the next day. It wasn't fair to be staying here with Jeff while the others did all the work. His mind was made up. He moved his blankets to the floor and promptly fell asleep.

Six

"HEY, HOFFLEBURGER! What the heck you doing down there?"

Billie pulled the blanket up over his eyes to keep the sun out, wondering why the forest was so bright and Charlie was calling him Hoffleburger. Then he realized it wasn't the forest but the floor of a house, and it wasn't Charlie, but Jeff. He rolled over and sat up.

Jeffrey Miller was still staring at him from the top bunk.

"What'd you do? Fall out of bed?"

Billie grinned, stretched, and plopped back down again. "Naw, bed's too soft, that's all."

Jeff laughed. "Man, you're something else, you know it? Now I'm *sure* I'm coming to visit you, if I have to put on my snorkel and fins and go underwater all the way."

"Better wait till we find a place," Billie told him.

He knew there would be no fish or biscuits for breakfast, and he had seen dry cereal in the grocery, but he didn't know the Millers ate it. Everybody had a bowl and spoon in front of him, and in the center of the table were several boxes, brightly colored, and a bunch of bananas. As Billie watched, everyone chose a box, filled his bowl full of small dry pieces that looked like wood shavings, poured milk over them, sprinkled on some sugar, and topped the whole mess with sliced banana.

Billie didn't think he could possibly eat it, but he tried. He picked up a box that said Shredded Wheat, and shook out a handful of pellets, just as Jeff was doing. Then he took a bite. His teeth sank into a hard, dry biscuit that tasted like string, and soon his mouth was full of little slivers while the milk ran down the back of his throat. He thought he would choke. He dared not swallow.

"How about some banana on top?" Mrs. Miller asked, and as soon as Billie opened his mouth to answer, the stuff went down, scratching and tickling all the way.

"You know," said Jeff's mother, "I don't think Billie cares for dry cereal, and I can't blame him." She took the bowl away and put it out on the porch for Gretchen, the dog, who lapped it greedily. Poor dog, thought Billie. "How would you like a waffle, Billie?"

81

"Me too!" yelled Keith, and suddenly everybody was clamoring for waffles. Whatever they were, Billie decided, they couldn't be worse.

Mrs. Miller took a package from the freezer and lifted out stiff slabs of something yellow with little dents all over them. Billie could not understand how these people stayed alive. Might as well cut up cardboard boxes and book covers to eat. But when he tasted the waffle, it was soft and warm, with melted butter and syrup on top, and he even ate another.

"What are you kids going to do today?" Mr. Miller asked. "Why don't you get your bike out, Jeff, and teach Billie to ride?"

"I think I'd better go back," Billie said quickly, though he would have loved the bike.

"You just got here," Jeff declared. "Heck, what's the hurry?"

"They'll need me to make a new camp," Billie told him. "I can hike over from here."

"I've got to drive down that way this morning. I'll drop you off," said Mr. Miller, "if you're sure you have to go."

"We could have had a lot of fun," said Jeff grumpily.

"Anyway, it's nice you could come for one night," said Mrs. Miller. "Maybe next time you can stay longer."

Jeff walked outside with Billie.

"I don't know why you have to go. Nobody sent for you," Jeff complained.

"But they need me. They're doing all the work. It wouldn't be fair."

Jeff gave him a playful punch on the arm. "Sometimes I wish you weren't so darn Indian! Sometimes, just once, I wish you'd do something just for yourself, just because you wanted to, without worrying about everybody else in your family. Heck, I mean, I've got feelings too! Worry about me for a change!"

They broke into laughter as Billie climbed into the truck beside Jeff's father.

"You've got the whole U.S. government looking after you," Billie quipped, and this time Mr. Miller joined in the laughter.

The truck backed down the drive and started up the street in the direction of the highway. Mr. Miller must have known what was going on in Billie's head because he said, "I suppose it's hard being away from your family when they need you. Things will be sort of rough for a while, I guess. But your father and uncle have been through it before. They'll manage. When you pick a new camp, let me know if you can use some help. I'm pretty good at sawing logs."

"Thanks," Billie smiled. "I'll tell my father."

"Jeff says you're doing pretty well in school, Billie. You like it?"

"Most of the time."

"Any idea how far you'd like to go?"

"Well . . . " Billie paused. "It changes, I guess. Sometimes I think about going on to high school. Maybe even college. And doing something with animals. And then sometimes I feel I'd like to go back to the island and just live the way my Grandfather does. I guess I'd like to do both."

"Maybe somehow you can. There are lots of different opportunities. There are people who go out and rescue animals and take care of them, people who study them, and people who write about them and draw or take pictures of them. And you know, Billie, whatever you do, you don't have to live in a house unless you want to—just something to keep in mind."

It was an idea Billie had never thought of before.

Billie got out on the other side of the highway from Mush Jim's boat shack, crossed over, and arrived in the middle of a big debate.

"It seems best for the rest of us, Sihoki," Tiger was saying in Mikasuki. "It's not what you wanted, I know, but Mush Jim and I checked out another island and the ground is even lower than the one we left. Water won't be down for several weeks at least. Besides, it would take us twice as long to get back and forth as it used to."

Billie sat down and listened. Despite the argument, nobody raised his voice. "Nobody is deaf, so why should we shout?" Grandfather used to say, comparing themselves to the tourists who hollered at each other at the service stations along the Trail.

"But the place you would take us is not even an island!" Sihoki protested. "It can be seen from the highway. Anyone may walk in!"

"We've got to go somewhere, Mother," Mush Jim said. "Tiger's got to get back to work. This way I wouldn't be leaving the dock all the time just to take the family back and forth. Billie can walk to camp from the bus stop when he gets home from school. He won't have to wait for me. And neither will Tiger or

Charlie. If we build and you don't like it after a time, we'll keep looking. If we find a place that's better—that's not so low—we'll move. What do you say?"

No one spoke while awaiting Sihoki's answer. It was her say and always had been. They were her pots, her kettles, her sewing machine. When she died, they would all become Alice Tommie's. But as long as she lived, Sihoki ruled the camp. If she could not live in the new place, they would keep looking.

She sat like a statue, her teeth clicking together as she thought. Like the old woman she was, she began to talk aloud to herself, wrestling with the decision: "Abraham and I could live a very long time with only a garden and chickens, so far to the south that only birds could find us. That would be peace. But now, with so many children, Tiger to work on the roads, Charlie to work in the fields, Mush Jim to his boat, Billie to school. . . . How can so many people going so many places live so far out on the water with so much going back and forth all the time?"

She stopped suddenly and looked over at her husband. For fifty summers they had shared the *sofkee* spoon. For fifty winters she had slept in his chickee and rubbed his back, made his gruel and cut his meat. How could she possibly answer without hearing from him, who was as much a part of her as her very arm?

"What do you say, Abraham?" she asked, and the look passed between them that Billie had seen so often, a gentle look.

"My heart is with the garden and the chickens," he

said. "But if we go back and the others stay, I do not know. Perhaps my heart stays here also."

"Then let us build in a new place," said Sihoki. "If Abraham and I do not learn to like it, we will go back to the old island. Then you will build us a chickee, and we will live our days in the old place. But first we will try."

And so it was settled.

The new place was a half mile west of Mush Jim's shanty. To get there, they crossed the canal on a footbridge made of two wooden planks, made their way through the dense undergrowth to a spot that was higher than the rest and surrounded by moss-covered trees. The ground was covered with pine needles, and it was cool, even in the heat of the day. There was a clearing of sorts, but of course, no chickees. Perhaps, in times past, it had been a hiding place for Osceola himself or Billy Bowlegs.

The land did not belong to the Tommie family, and it was not on a reservation. But whatever the land was, state property or privately owned, it was hardly useful for anything else. In many places along the Tamiami Trail, the Indians lived in "squatter camps." They did not own the land they lived on, but nobody really cared that they stayed.

There was a lot to be done. Trees had to be cut down to make the space larger, and brush cleared away for a garden. Working together, Tiger and Mush Jim cut the trees into posts for the chickees, and Abraham began staking them out. Jeff's father came as he had offered and helped saw logs for a day. As the week went on, relatives from Big Cypress—John Jumper and Dan Gopher, came to help thatch the palmetto fronds for the roofs, breaking the fronds with a hatchet. The thatch had to be cut fresh every day so that it would be green and flexible. Mush Jim made sure that Billie and Charlie helped some with each step, so that when they were grown, they could build a complete chickee themselves if necessary.

Billie knew that when the chickees were finished here, Tiger and Mush Jim would go to Big Cypress in turn to help build up what the hurricane had torn apart there. No one had to be asked for his help. What kind of man would not go where he was needed?

It was more than a week before things were in order and the men could go back to work. When the last box and kettle had been carried across the footbridge and through the tall grass to the camp, the sky was bright and the birds were singing. The ground was drying out and the alligators and rabbits had come out of hiding. The clothes which Alice Tommie and Grandmother had salvaged from the trees and bushes were damp with mildew, and everything needed washing, even the bedding. While the men loaded the family's possessions into the pickup truck and brought them to the new chickees, Sihoki and Alice took the children and went to the bank on the east side of the camp to wash.

Billie and Charlie took off their clothes and plunged in, scrubbing their bodies with the soap that Mother handed them and laughing at the dog who was snapping at the bubbles. But Grandmother and Alice and Watsie went about it another way. They simply waded in and sat down in the water, clothes and all, washing their bodies and their clothes at the same time, and draped the extra clothes they had washed over bushes to dry.

"Charlie, do you know what the Millers eat for breakfast?" Billie said, remembering. "That cereal that comes in boxes. It looks like string and tastes like pieces of books all chopped up. Really!"

"And if white peoples come to this camp, they will bring their box food with them, and Watsie will eat it," Sihoki grumbled. "It is like gravel in the stomach. It makes—Ei!"

Grandmother shrieked so suddenly that Billie dropped the soap. When he turned around, he saw three tourists who had hiked across the footbridge and through the grass, and were snapping pictures as boldly as if the Tommie family were animals in a zoo.

"Ei!" Sihoki cried again, turning her back to them.

"Get one of the little girl!" a woman in slacks kept urging the man beside her. "And the old woman!"

"This place is ours! You are in our camp!" Billie said, ducking down in the water beside Charlie.

"My Lord, the kid speaks English!" the man said.

"Hurry, George, and snap that thing before they go away!" the woman insisted, and Billie knew he had to do something.

Like fish flashing in the water, his arms began beating on the surface, sending a wall of spray into the air that rose thick and foamy between him and the tourists.

"See!" a second woman bellowed. "You waited too long! Now look what those fool kids are doing!"

Faster and faster went Billie's arms, and then Charlie joined in with his feet, hiding Alice Tommie and Watsie and Sihoki behind the foam.

"They're getting my camera wet!" the man cried disgustedly.

Just then Tiger came down the path. Billie stopped splashing and watched. His father stood straight and stiff, unmoving, and the tourists stopped uneasily.

"Just. . . uh. . . wanted to get some pictures," the man explained.

"This is our home," Tiger said, and still did not move.

"Hey, listen, we weren't going to *take* anything," the man said soothingly.

"I do not come into your home," Tiger said, and waited.

"Well. . . I'm. . . I'm sorry." A red flush crept up the man's neck and over his cheeks.

Tiger stood aside and the group passed. They went directly to the footbridge and on out to the road again.

Billie and Charlie began giggling and splashing each other. But Sihoki did not think it funny and sat there in the water shaking her head and slowly scrubbing at her skirt.

"Like vultures they will come into camp, clicking, clicking, always clicking their little black boxes. They

89

will peer in the chickees and lift the lid of the cooking pot. What manners these people have! How shall we live in this place?"

Seven

IT WAS not quite the same as the camp on the island, surrounded by the night sounds they knew so well, lulled to sleep by the bark of the fox, watched over by the owl, and wakened by the morning call of the limpkin.

Now they went to sleep to the noise of the cars and trucks on the Tamiami Trail. The new camp was situated on a peninsula of sorts which jutted out into the north side of the swamp. Here they were but a few yards from the water which surrounded them on three sides, and a quarter mile from the highway. Trees hid most of the camp from tourists on the

Tamiami Trail, but if someone looked hard enough, he could make out the edge of the cookhouse in the clearing, and if he stopped his car and crossed the footbridge, making his way through the tall grass, he would have no trouble finding the camp.

This side of the swamp was not the lagoon they had loved so well on the far island. Here other airboats roared up and down the canal, and once or twice a day an airboat filled with tourists would slowly skirt the camp shattering the quiet. At these times Alice and Sihoki would move back into the shadows, out of range of the cameras.

Billie could never get used to the tourists, no matter where he saw them. Sometimes when he and Charlie went to the Indian souvenir store with Mush Jim on Saturdays, a tourist would come up to him and say, "Hey, young fella, are you a full-fledged Indian?" If Mush Jim were listening, Billie would have to say, "yes," and the tourist would ask him to pose for a picture.

If Mush Jim weren't listening, however, when the tourists asked Billie that question, he would stare at them blankly and say in Mikasuki, "No, I am a buffalo." They would think he couldn't understand English. Then he and Charlie would giggle and move around and jiggle so that the tourists couldn't get any pictures at all.

Of course, not all the tourists who traveled the Trail were like that. Some just smiled at Billie in a friendly way and didn't try to find out his name or make him do stupid things for a nickle or ask dumb questions like, didn't he think it was time he did a little dance and brought on some rain? There were even some whom Billie wished he could get to know better, but most of them he never saw again.

Occasionally Alice Tommie would look up from the sewing machine to see a group of tourists making their way across the footbridge, eager to explore, eyes open wide, looking for real Indians.

Once Sihoki was working at the high table beside the cookhouse, chopping meat and drying it in the sun, when a tall woman in a blue hat asked what was in the stewpan and whether or not she could taste it.

"Ye gods!" the woman had exclaimed, looking around at the dirty pots sitting in pans of water. "Did you ever see such unsanitary conditions?"

They never understood that Seminoles wash their dishes just before they use them, not after, and that the Indians consider themselves much cleaner than the American housewife who lets her dishes accumulate dust in the cupboard and then uses them at mealtime without washing them first.

Tiger Tommie taught Alice to say, "Excuse me, this is our home," when tourists came into camp, and often this would bring a quick apology and they would leave immediately, embarrassed. But sometimes it only sent them scattering in all directions taking as many pictures as they could before they were forced to go.

Finally Mush Jim put up a sign that said, "Beware of Dog," and when that didn't work, he took it down and put up another. Only Mush Jim knew what the words meant. They were even too difficult for Billie. But the sign worked magic, for the tourists would come only as far as the post halfway between the bridge and the camp, see the sign, stop, and then beat a hasty retreat. So Billie copied down the words and took them to school to show his science teacher.

"Cholera! Good grief, Billie! Where did you see that sign?"

"It's on a post by our camp," Billie said.

"What? Who put it there? When?"

"Mush Jim. My uncle. A friend gave it to him. Said it would keep the tourists away."

Mr. Bernard stared at Billie and then began to laugh. "I'll bet it does, too! It says, 'Cholera. Quarantine. Department of Public Health.' That means there is a dangerous disease in your camp, and no one is to enter until the inspector takes the sign down." He chuckled again. "How is the new camp, Billie?"

"It's a lot easier now for Dad and Mush Jim to get to their jobs," Billie said.

"I hope it works out then. The storm was hard on a lot of folks this time, and the Seminoles were hardest hit. I'm glad you found another place."

Mr. Bernard was great. It was a sure thing that none of his ancestors had been related to General Thompson. As for Mrs. Kelly, all she had said to Billie when he came back to school in mid-October was, "If you take any more time off, Billie, I'll need a note from your father." She didn't even ask why he had missed school or whether the camp was done.

Welcome back, Jeff had written on the blackboard,

hidden under the calendar at one end. *Kelly's been having cat-fits 'cause you've been out of school so long.*

Always knew she wasn't human, Billie wrote in reply.

Billie tried to spend more time than usual with his grandfather. Even though Abraham and Sihoki had a chickee just like they had before, it didn't seem the same somehow to the old man. The sun which rose now above the trees on the Tamiami Trail seemed different from the sun which had awakened him each morning in the forest, its rays filtering through the dense leaves of the cypress and falling softly on his face. Even the birds sounded different.

One afternoon, Billie was working on a diagram of the earth's crust on the floor of the chickee, his school paints in front of him. Abraham had begun his carvings again for the souvenir shop, but he worked slower than usual, stopped frequently, and his heart seemed to be somewhere else.

By the time Billie finished his drawing, there was paint on his arms and face, paint on Watsie who crawled around over his back, and even a dab on the dog.

"Hey, look, Grandfather. I'm a warrior!" Billie said, pointing to the paint on his face.

Grandfather looked up and grunted. It was too much for a self-respecting Seminole. He went back to his carving.

"Remember the wheel you used to paint, Grandfather—the wheel of life?" Billie asked. "Paint one for me, would you?"

"It takes work," said Abraham.

"Please!"

"You would forget it."

"No, I wouldn't. I'll memorize it so I can show it to my own children some day."

"You would lose it. The pigs would walk upon it."

"No, Grandfather. I'll put it away carefully and keep it forever. I promise. I could even take it to school and show the class!" Mr. Bernard's class, of course, not Mrs. Kelly's. He took a sheet of drawing paper from his folder and placed it before Abraham.

"All right," Grandfather agreed. "This is the last one I will make. You must listen carefully so you do not forget."

After picking up one of Billie's brushes, Grandfather drew a large red circle and divided it into four equal parts. Just outside the red circle he drew a blue one. Beyond the blue one he drew a black one, beyond the black a yellow circle, and outside the yellow, a white one, the largest of all.

"It is the wheel of life," said Grandfather. "Red means that a man is well. Blood red. Blue—When a man is struck sick, his skin turns blue. Black—Blood turns black when a man dies. Yellow—When a man is dead, his bones turn yellow. And white—When a man is dead a long time, the flesh is all gone; the bones are white.

"The red-spoked wheel represents the earth with the well man standing in the center of it," Abraham explained. "But when he gets sick, his soul wanders the color paths of the wheel. Spirits of the dead lure the man's ghost on while the medicine man calls it back. Should it reach the east, however, the man dies, and his soul goes west by way of the red spoke to the village of the dead."

Billie listened quietly, trying to memorize the story he'd heard before but not quite remembered.

"How does the medicine man call him back, Grandfather?"

"When a man gets sick, his body shakes. The medicine man sings. He calls the ghost back. He blows on a pipe. He goes after the ghost and brings it back. The man gets well."

"What will happen, Grandfather, when there aren't any medicine men left?"

It was a subject that Abraham didn't like to talk about.

"Not good, not good," he murmured, shaking his head. "The young forget the old ways. Everybody is too busy. Nobody learns the secret of the medicine bundle. Some day many people will get sick. Nobody will know the medicine. It is not good."

Little as Billie knew about Seminole medicine, he realized instinctively the danger in losing all the old ways that Grandfather talked about. There was no question in his mind that the medicine men could heal. Tiger himself, who was no medicine man but had learned much from his father, had doctored the family as long as Billie could remember. Several times Tiger had taken his sons to the medicine man and they had been cured by his medicine. Only once had the medicine man suggested they go to the white man's clinic, and that was when Watsie had an infection in her eyes.

But now the few remaining medicine men were old, and no one was prepared to take their place. There was a time, five years before, when Abraham had held Billie on his knee and announced that Billie would perhaps be the next medicine man. But then, when Billie started school in the white man's world, Abraham said nothing more about it, and Billie seemed to know deep down that he would not become a medicine man. And if he didn't, would he still be able to walk the sky path when he died? Would he be Indian enough to find the way?

Grandfather must have been thinking the same thing, for he was very quiet, and his profile stood out sharply against the sunlight beyond the chickee.

"Listen, Grandfather, let me draw something for you now. Sit just like that—don't move—and I'll draw your picture."

Billie took his pencil and began sketching the old man's profile—the tuft of white hair, the straight forehead, the long proud nose, the thin lips, the chin. Pretty good, if he did say so himself.

He smiled as he worked. Now he was drawing the back of the head, the wisps of hair that hung down around the ears, and the kerchief that Grandfather wore knotted about his neck. He turned the paper carefully as he worked, and the old man sat so still that Billie thought he had gone to sleep. A pretty good likeness of Grandfather, Billie decided. Maybe he'd take it to school and show it to Jeff. But when he put his pencil down finally, Grandfather said, "Now I want to see it."

Abraham held the paper far away from his face. He looked at it carefully and then at Billie. "It is me," he said, surprised. "Then I will keep it. And I give you the wheel of life. It is a present from an old man to his grandson. May you stand in the center of the wheel until you are very old, like Abraham."

There was a kind of understanding that when the water went down and the ground dried out, Abraham and Sihoki would go back to the old island and Mush Jim would build a chickee for them there. At times Billie toyed with the idea of going with them. He could drop out of school and spend the time hoeing their garden, fishing with Grandfather, and doing all the chores that they were getting too old to do themselves. He felt this way the most when he sat in the chickee beside Abraham each evening. But as soon as he got to school the next day, studying about places he had never been and people he had never seen and things he had never done, he felt a tug away from the quiet camp and into the big world beyond.

Alice and Tiger and Mush Jim liked the convenience of the new camp, but they knew the old folks were not happy so close to the Tamiami Trail. So they all waited for the water to recede on the far island, and yet, when it did, nobody asked Sihoki and Abraham about leaving. Abraham would say, "When we go home . . ." or Sihoki would say, "When I get back to the old cookhouse. . . ." They never really suggested going, however. And so the weeks went by. Everybody seemed to be waiting for time itself to make the decision. No one wanted the old people to leave, Billie least of all.

Mush Jim was working now on whatever jobs he could find. He helped repair houses and stores and gas stations along the highway which had been hit by the hurricane, and even agreed to wrestle alligators every Saturday at one and three o'clock in the Indian Village and Souvenir Shop on the Trail. It was a job he did not enjoy, but he needed the money. Tiger wouldn't have wrestled alligators even if he were starving to death. And Grandfather thought it to be completely unnecessary. There were vegetables in the garden, fish in the water, rabbits and squirrels in the woods, and what more could a Seminole want? He could not understand his son's interest in money, and when Mush Jim explained that he needed money to buy gasoline for the truck, repairs on the airboat, shoes and boots and tools and tee shirts, Grandfather waved it away with one brown hand and said they were not worth it. If he were Mush Jim, he would sell his possessions at the first auction, and go off to live in the peace of the forest.

Billie went along with his uncle one Saturday for the alligator wrestling and was surprised to see Jeff Miller standing in front of the souvenir store eating an ice cream bar.

"Hey, Jeff!" he said. "What are you doing here?"

"What do you think? Eating ice cream," Jeff grinned.

"You mean you walked all the way over?"

"No, Dad brought me on his way to Naples. I'll have to walk home, but it's better than sitting around the house all day. What are you doing?"

"My uncle's going to wrestle an alligator at one o'clock. Then . . ." He shrugged. "Go home, I guess."

"Live far from here?"

"No, not too."

"Then I'm coming along." Jeff said it so definitely that Billie knew he would. Well, he'd let him and see what happened.

They went inside the Indian Village, back of the store, and over to the alligator pit where tourists were already gathered, cameras ready. Mush Jim crawled over the wall of the pit, barefoot, and took off his shirt. He wasn't smiling. He didn't even look at the crowd that was watching him. Picking up a pole, he prodded the big beast that lay in the sun and the alligator turned and hissed loudly. The lady cashier from the store came outside.

"Good afternoon," she said pleasantly to the small crowd. "The Indian Village and Souvenir Shop is pleased to present one of our finest alligator wrestlers, Mush Jim, for your entertainment. Our wrestlers are not paid for their work, so you may show your appreciation at the end of the demonstration by placing a contribution in the cups provided along the wall."

Jeff leaned over the wall and watched as Mush Jim grappled the huge 'gator whose tail was now thrashing hard against the ground.

Into the water they went, Mush Jim clinging to the alligator's back, and disappeared in the murky pool. Bubbles came up, then the alligator's thrashing tail, and finally, when the tourists began gasping in astonishment at the way he was holding his breath, Mush Jim rose up, gulping for air, with the alligator's head locked firmly in his arms, jaws gripped tightly closed.

"I've always wondered how they do it," Jeff whispered to Billie. "Is it a trick?"

Billie shook his head.

Mush Jim eased the alligator out of the pool, belly up, still holding the jaws shut. Slowly the 'gator's eyes glazed and closed, the tail stopped lashing, the legs went limp. Mush Jim opened its fierce jaws and held them wide for a brief moment.

Then he stood up, making strange noises in his throat, quick grunting sounds. Hearing the noises, the alligator began kicking again, and finally rolled over on its stomach and crawled off in one corner.

The tourists clapped, Jeff along with them.

"Putting an alligator on its back knocks him out," Billie explained. "But when he hears a noise like another 'gator, it usually brings him out of it. If not, Mush Jim turns him over."

The crowd was going away now. Some dropped a quarter or two in the cups along the wall. One man in a straw hat handed Mush Jim a dollar bill. "Good show," he said. Mush Jim counted the change in the cups. Altogether he'd been paid two dollars and seventy cents. That was all.

"Boy, I wouldn't wrestle a 'gator for a thousand dollars!" Jeff said. "Is it a secret how you do it, Mush Jim?"

Mush Jim wiped his face with his shirt. "No secret, Jeff. You have to know a little about alligators, that's all. It's hard work to hold its mouth open, but hardly anything to hold it closed. Just the way the muscles work. And of course, you have to watch out for the tail."

"Maybe I'll wrestle them someday," said Billie.

Mush Jim jerked around. "No, you won't. I'm the last alligator wrestler in the family." He talked like he meant it. "You're the new Indian—and you don't have to do things like this. That's why you're going to school—so you'll learn something else."

Billie thought about it as they walked out to the front of the shop. "The new Indian," Mush Jim had called him. He'd never heard that said before. Abraham, Tiger, and Mush Jim were all different sorts of Indians, and now he was different in still another way. Which of the four was the real Mikasuki? Which would Osceola choose if he were here again?

"What are you going to do now?" Mush Jim asked. He bought them each a Coke and leaned against the store, letting the sun dry his soaking jeans.

"I don't know. Stick around and watch your three o'clock show, I guess," Billie said.

"I think one is enough. You've got better things to

do than just hang around. Go home and keep Abraham company. You stand here and you'll end up posing for tourists all afternoon."

"Okay," said Billie. "See you later, then."

Mush Jim went inside the store to talk to the sales girls and Billie turned to go.

"Well, I'm ready," Jeff said, clunking his empty bottle down in the case beside the door. "Which way?"

Billie stared at him in amazement. What nerve! Billie could never barge in another camp, knowing he was unwelcome, in a million years. He grinned. "Jeff, you're nuts! You really are!"

"Why? What'll your family do? Sic the dog on me?"

Billie laughed. "The dog will take one look at you and run away. He'll think you're a dead man walking, with white skin and yellow bones."

"Okay," said Jeff. "The first friend I'm going to make is the dog."

Eight

IT WAS the dog who heard them coming first, crossing the narrow footbridge and winding through the tall grass on the other side.

"Here, dog, come on, dog, let's be buddies," Jeff said, stooping down and holding out his hand to the barking animal.

"Be still," Billie said to the dog, and it stayed close beside him. Warily it let Jeff approach, and after a bit, Jeff was patting its head.

"See?" said Jeff. "It's easy."

"You'll never get past Grandmother that way," Billie grinned. "But you like to find out the hard way."

They continued up the winding path till they came to the clearing. The moment Sihoki heard them, she turned around. Seeing Billie's friend, she raised her arms and uttered a long string of words in Mikasuki.

Her language was so bewildering that Jeff stopped in his tracks. What Grandmother was saying was, "Ei! First a pilot, then the tourists, now a white-faced boy! Like a horde of locusts they are upon us and soon we shall eat and dress and sleep before the world!" But to Jeff it seemed as though she were saying, "Don't take one more step, young man," and so he waited uncomfortably for the torrent to stop.

Tiger and Alice had taken Watsie to the clinic to have her eyes checked. Charlie had gone with them, and only the old folks remained in camp.

"Grandmother," Billie said, speaking in Mikasuki. "This is Jeff Miller, my friend from school. His father buys our frogs. Can he stay for a little while?"

"Do you think I will chase him away?" Sihoki cried angrily. "First you bring him, *then* you ask!"

"He wanted to come. He's been asking for a long time."

"He has no home? No family? What does he want of us but to gawk at my kettle and step on my skirts? Bah!" And Sihoki turned her back and started the hand-operated sewing machine again at full speed.

It was an embarrassing situation. What should he do now, Billie wondered. Send Jeff away? Take him on in?

"Billie."

Grandfather was standing off to one side, throwing feed to the chickens. His old eyes twinkled, and he motioned Billie over. "Leave your grandmother in peace. Show your friend around camp. Let her watch from the corner of her eye and get used to him slowly."

So Billie showed Jeff around the camp, avoiding Sihoki's chickee. He showed him the garden where the pumpkins and squash and cane were growing, the baby pigs that had been born of the sow they had saved, and the new hens scratching in the bare earth under the chickees. All the while Sihoki stared at the white visitor with glowering eyes, turning her head abruptly whenever the boy looked at her and harrumphing at Abraham for inviting him in.

"What manners!" she muttered under her breath. "What rudeness!"

But Jeff made no move to leave. He wanted to stay and do whatever Billie did when he was home, and Sihoki's ire began to rise even more. If there was one thing she disliked even more than strangers in the camp, it was being ignored. Faster and faster the sewing machine went, and louder and louder her voice, as though she were talking to Billie directly. Grandfather's idea was not working.

"What's she saying?" Jeff whispered.

Billie smiled. "She says your eyes are like a hawk's. You look at everything."

The old woman mumbled on. And minutes later Jeff asked again, "Now what's she saying?"

"She says she wonders if you are ever going to leave

or if you are going to sleep in our beds," Billie grinned. "Listen, Jeff, quit asking. You should have heard her the night we picked up the pilot!"

But it bothered Jeff that he was so unwelcome. Grandmother didn't even know him, so how could she dislike him? He was sure they could be friends if she'd give him a chance. She stole longer and longer glances at him, clicking her teeth and glaring, and he felt that things would only get worse unless he thought of something quickly.

As Jeff neared the cookhouse, Sihoki cried out, "Now he takes the food from our mouths!" And suddenly Jeff sat down on a bench near the fire, held his stomach, and started moaning.

"Jeff! Hey! What's the matter?" Billie cried, as the dog scurried away, tail between his legs, and Grandmother stopped chattering in mid-sentence.

Billie stooped down beside Jeff, but the boy continued to moan.

"Ei!" cried Grandmother, dropping the skirt she was sewing. "What is the matter?"

"I don't know," said Billie, frightened himself. "Jeff, what's wrong?"

"Ohhhaaawwww!" Jeff moaned.

Grandmother came hobbling over, beating her sides as she came.

"What does he say?" asked Grandmother, frightened, unable to understand a word.

Billie stared at Jeff in bewilderment. "He's got a horrible pain in his stomach, I guess."

Jeff was moaning again. "Food. . . I can't go another step. I'm starving to death."

"Starving!" Billie croaked. "What the heck are you talking about? You just had ice cream, peanuts, and a Coke!"

"What? What?" cried Grandmother.

"He needs food, I guess. That's what he says."

"So feed him!" Grandmother cried, hurrying over to the stew pot. This would have to happen today, with Mush Jim gone. A starving boy in camp, and no wonder, the way those mothers fed their children out of boxes! How could a boy grow fat on that?

She filled a bowl with stew and blew at it. When it was cool enough to eat, she pressed the spoon to Jeff's lips. "There, there," she said in Mikasuki. "*Here* is food that fills the stomach."

Billie stared in disbelief. What an act! What nerve! That nutty guy!

"Oohhhaaawww!" Jeff cried again when the spoonful was gone, and Sihoki quickly handed him the bowl so that he could feed himself.

Jeff slowly put another bite to his lips and then another, rolling it around a little before he swallowed, and then gulping it down quickly, as though it were burning a hole in his throat. When he was half through, he set the bowl down beside him. "Delicious!" he said to Grandmother. "The best I've ever tasted."

"What does he say?" inquired Grandmother.

"He says that it's the best he's ever tasted," Billie told her.

"Then eat! Eat!" Sihoki cried, and thrust the bowl back in Jeff's hands.

Billie turned away to hide his face. He was struggling to keep from laughing. Jeff couldn't possibly eat all that after the junk he'd had at the Indian Village. But he'd brought it on himself. He was playing on Sihoki's sympathy, and now he'd have to get himself out of it.

Slowly Jeff began to eat the second half of the bowl, belching politely in his hand and struggling to get the bites down. Finally he was through.

"Billie," he groaned. "Please tell her I have to rest—that she's the best cook in the world, but I still have to rest."

Billie translated what Jeff had said.

"Bah!" said Sihoki, but she was pleased.

The boys had not reckoned with Grandfather, however. Throughout the whole performance, Abraham had watched, puzzled, from the back of the chickee. He caught the looks and winks and giggles that Sihoki had missed. Slowly he got up and came over, and when Billie looked at his face, he knew at once what Grandfather thought of the whole trick.

Abraham's voice was patient. "Billie," he said, "tell your friend I am very sorry he was taken sick with hunger." He waited. Billie repeated it to Jeff.

"Tell your friend we are glad he liked the meat we cook. It will make his body strong."

With a sinking heart, Billie repeated it to Jeff, who nodded and smiled at Grandfather. Jeff obviously did not know what was coming.

"Tell your friend it is not an Indian custom to send a stranger away sick and weak, that he should stay until he has eaten another bowlful of meat and is much stronger."

"I don't think he has time to stay and eat any m . . . more, Grandfather," Billie stammered.

"He has time," said Grandfather.

Billie repeated it to Jeff, whose eyes widened. He had eaten ice cream, Coke, pretzels and two bags of potato chips before he started out for camp, not to mention his lunch, and now he watched sickeningly as Grandfather himself removed the lid of the cooking pot. Up came a heaping spoonful of meat. Abraham started to add another, but thought better of it and stopped, handing the bowl to Jeff.

"You are welcome to our food," he said. "May it make strong blood."

Billie translated it almost inaudibly. Slowly Jeff began to eat. Sihoki smiled. She enjoyed being a good cook. Now the white boy with the skinny arms would return to his funny house with walls and tell his young mother what good food was really like. Grandfather sat across from Jeff, looking serenely out over the swamp, and Billie stood silently by, miserable.

The bowl was finished at last. Jeff unfastened his belt, and groaned in earnest. "Billie," he burped, "I think I'd better go."

"Sure you've had enough to eat?" Billie couldn't resist asking.

Jeff put his hand over his mouth and started for the path.

Abraham stood up. "Billie, tell your friend he is welcome here again," he said, and added, eyes twinkling, "One need not use tricks to make friends."

Billie followed his friend back out to the footbridge, and as soon as they were beyond the post, Jeff said, "What the heck does your grandmother put in that stew!" As soon as the words were out, the boys shrieked with laughter, big belly laughs that exploded from one and then the other.

"Spice, brother, spice!" said Billie. "Serves you right. You didn't have Grandfather fooled for a minute."

Jeff stared at him. "You mean. . .you mean he *knew*? Now I feel like an idiot. I really do. I was only trying to make friends with her. I couldn't think of anything else."

"Don't worry. She wants you to come back—wants to feed you properly."

"I'm too embarrassed now," said Jeff.

But Jeff wasn't embarrassed for long. The following week he stopped by again after school, and Billie introduced him to Tiger and Alice and Charlie. And the Thursday after that, Billie brought Jeff home with him to spend the night so he could go frogging with them.

It was a new experience having a white friend in the camp. Every Friday he would hear the other boys talking about who was going to whose house for dinner or to spend the night or just play ball, and Billie used to wonder what it would be like to invite somebody other than cousins from Big Cypress— somebody new.

Charlie was shy. He always was shy with strangers. But it was hard to be shy around Jeff Miller for long. When the boys started a game of volley ball, Charlie began to laugh out loud at the crazy way Jeff butted the ball with his head.

"Where did you learn to play like that?" Charlie called.

"Comes natural. My granddaddy was a mountain goat," Jeff said, giving it an extra hard butt which sent it bouncing off across the clearing, the dog chasing it joyously.

Watsie watched wide-eyed from the corner of one chickee where she clutched her doll, and Grandmother busied herself with the evening meal. She and Alice ran cubes of meat onto a palmetto spear, roasting them hard and dry to be cooked with rice and tomatoes. Mother smiled as she watched Billie and Charlie playing with their new friend. It was good to see Charlie smile and good to see him make friends.

When it was time for dinner, Jeff sat with the others. He dutifully swallowed down his food, being careful to leave a little on his plate so they would not add more.

As darkness fell, the boys prepared to go frogging. Jeff was offered one of Billie's long-sleeved jackets to keep mosquitoes off his arms, and he chose the one with the red and yellow stripes.

It was a warm night for November. With spears and buckets, the three boys set out in the airboat toward the lagoon in the mangrove swamp where the frogs swam about in the water or sat on the rocks, croaking their grumpy night songs. Jeff looked all around, wide-eyed, as though at any moment creatures of the swamp might rise up out of the dark water and surprise him.

Slowly the boat moved in on the rocks where the

frogs sat transfixed as the light overpowered them. Billie nodded to Charlie when he had the light trained just so. *Whup!* Charlie moved so swiftly that the suddenness of his throw startled Jeff. Instantly the spear was retrieved with a frog on the end of it, and again the spear flashed out in the gleam of the light and got another.

"Can I try?" Jeff shouted. Billie cut off the motor.

"Hold it like this," he said, showing Jeff how to grip the spear. "Aim it, and throw."

"Now!" said Charlie.

Jeff stood for a moment, aiming it carefully as he had seen Charlie do, then—*whup.*

It happened so quickly that none of the boys knew quite how, but somehow Jeff went along with the spear and a moment later was sprawling over the side of the boat and into the two-foot deep water as the boat bobbed back and forth and the frogs scattered in all directions.

Billie looked over the side of the boat to see Jeff groping up out of the mud, and he threw back his head in a shriek of laughter.

Suddenly it turned to a scream. There was a roaring hiss from the trees on the bank, and an alligator rushed toward them. Even before Billie had seen the length of the tail and the monstrous body, he knew it was the Big One. He remembered that peculiar deep hiss, that seemed to shake the flesh off one's bones, like wind in a cavern. He yelled at Jeff to get into the boat.

With lightning speed the huge 'gator came crashing through the underbrush, the wind rushing out of the huge cavernous mouth with rows and rows of dagger teeth, and the boys screamed together in terror, Jeff loudest of all as he tried to get to his feet in the muck.

"The light, Billie, the light!" Charlie yelled, scrambling to get the motor started again.

Never had Billie's fingers felt so much like thumbs. Desperately he struggled to turn the light in the eyes of the beast, but it didn't seem to move. Frantically he picked up a spear, just as Jeff dived headlong into the boat, one muddy foot kicking Billie's hand and knocking the spear into the water. With a roar the motor caught and rose higher and higher as the airboat tipped this way and that and Charlie tried to get it pointed into open water again.

The Big One charged. *Whop*, went the tail against the side of the boat, and the small craft spun crazily around, as though it were caught in a whirlpool. *Whop*, went the tail again, and the boys fell against each other.

Again Billie grabbed the light and this time it pivoted directly into the alligator's eyes. The monster seemed to freeze in confusion, still hissing, and then, from behind the huge animal, in the light of the lamp, came a small baby 'gator slithering under its mother's belly, and then another.

"Billie!" Charlie yelled above the noise of the engine. "Look! Baby 'gators!"

"The Big One's a mother!" Billy screamed back.

But Jeff didn't care if she was the great-grandmother of all the alligators in the Everglades. All he wanted to do was get away. With a roar the boat took off full speed, and moments later they were far out in the middle of the lagoon.

There was a lot of talk in camp that night, and Jeff felt good to be a part of it.

"I'll get Beets Fraser tomorrow, and we'll go see if we can scare her out again," said Mush Jim. "Like to size her up and see if she's really as big as I thought. Looked a good fifteen feet to me, the time I saw her, but they don't come that big often."

"Good place to stay away from till those babies are grown," Tiger warned his sons. "Nothing as fierce as a mother 'gator protecting her young. May be eighteen months before it's safe to go along that bank again. Do your gigging on the other side."

Charlie helped rig up a muslin canopy for Jeff at bedtime, but none of them felt sleepy. There was too much to talk about.

"Know what?" Jeff confessed, as the three boys lay on their backs in the chickee looking out at the dark sky. "That was the scaredest I've been in my whole life! I mean, *really* scared. It makes me shiver to think about it."

"I was scared too," said Charlie. "I tried to start the motor and it wouldn't kick."

"Well, I'm glad you waited till I got back in the boat," Jeff told him, and they laughed. "Listen, I wish you guys would come with Dad and me to Miami sometime. How about it? Did you ever go swimming on the beach? Or see the Seaquarium? We could have a great time."

It made Billie feel good that Charlie was included, and he realized how few friends his brother had. Where did Charlie have a chance to meet anybody? Most of the Indians who worked the fields were older than he. Other boys his age were in school. If the Tommies hadn't lived out on the island so long, perhaps Tiger would have enrolled Charlie in school too. When he finally had made up his mind to enroll Billie, Charlie was already eleven, and far too shy even to consider going. Maybe that's the way it had been with Mush Jim. Billie didn't like the thought of Charlie working the fields or wrestling alligators on and on forever and never being able to do anything else.

But then he looked over at Grandfather who was walking slowly around the clearing, poking at the underbrush with his stick, inspecting the pumpkins, listening to the sounds of the birds as they settled down for the night. Was this such a bad life? Would he ever have wanted Grandfather to be any different? Did Charlie, himself, want to be one of the "new Indians" that Mush Jim talked about? Billie didn't know.

As for himself, he liked having Jeff as a friend. He liked going places and learning things. But he wanted something Indian to come back to when the day was over. Sometimes he felt he was caught between two cultures, and other times he wondered if he couldn't have a little of each.

"I'll ask Mother if we can go to Miami sometime," Billie promised. "It sounds great."

The night noises grew louder now—the frogs they hadn't caught and the birds in the cluster of trees around them.

"Man, how do you guys sleep on these hard boards?" Jeff moaned as he tried to settle down under his canopy and brought the whole thing flopping down over his head.

Charlie and Billie hung it back up for him, laughing. "All it takes is a little more fat on those bones," said Billie dryly. "All you need is a couple more bowls of Grandmother's stew."

"Good night!" Jeff said quickly, and a moment later he added, "If I can't get to sleep, I don't even have a floor to lie on, do I, Billie?"

"You're on it," said Billie, and he went to sleep grinning.

Nine

BILLIE had never stolen anything in his life. Everything that was in the camp belonged to them all and was shared alike. If one of the brothers received a present, it was simply understood that the present belonged to the other also. So when the idea came to Billie to borrow a book from school and take it to Charlie, it did not cross his mind that some might consider this stealing.

He got the idea when he was in the school library on Monday. He found the book on training horses that Charlie had liked so much, and decided to check it out and take it home to read to his brother. And then, right beside it, he found another horse book, *Misty*, and he knew Charlie would like that even more. He'd take them both home, and maybe Charlie would get so interested that he'd really try hard to learn to read this time. But when Billie tried to sign them out, the librarian said, "Only one book each. You'll have to put one of these back for some other time."

All morning Billie thought about it. It wasn't fair, because the books weren't for him, they were for Charlie. Think of all the weeks and years that Charlie hadn't had any books at all! Next week, maybe, *Misty* would be gone. Someone else would check it out, and Billie might not have another chance for a long time.

So he decided to borrow it secretly. He would take good care of the book, and as soon as Charlie learned to read, he would bring it back. At lunch time, when the children finished eating and swarmed into the library or out to the playground, Billie went back to the shelf, slipped the book inside his notebook, and started out the door.

He felt a hand on his shoulder and stopped. Miss Ames, the librarian, was looking down at him and her face was serious.

"Just a minute, Billie," she said. "Open your notebook, please."

Billie quickly opened the notebook. It seemed so fair, he was sure she would understand when he explained it to her, but she didn't even ask.

"I want you to come with me," she said. "We're going to have a talk with your teacher."

120

Not Mrs. Kelly! Billie's heart sank. He knew what she would think. She'd say that was all she could expect from the great-great-grandson of a man who might have killed General Thompson. His face felt hot as he followed the librarian down the hall and into the room where Mrs. Kelly was writing the afternoon arithmetic on the blackboard.

"Mrs. Kelly," said Miss Ames, and her voice was stern. "We have a problem here."

Mrs. Kelly looked at Billie and came over slowly.

"This morning, this young man tried to check out two books on horses and I explained to him that he was allowed only one. Just now, I found him trying to sneak *Misty* out of the library, hidden in his notebook."

"Is this true, Billie?" asked Mrs. Kelly softly, and her eyes searched his face.

Of course it was true. Hadn't she heard? He nodded, angry at both of them.

Miss Ames took *Misty* away from Billie. "I'm not in the business of punishing pupils, so I'll leave him to you. But I can't let my books be stolen."

"Thanks for coming to me," Mrs. Kelly said. "I guess it's something I should know."

They were alone in the room together, and Billie wished she'd hurry and say it. He knew what she was thinking. What was she waiting for?

"Has this ever happened before, Billie?" she asked finally.

He shook his head.

"Then why now? What's so great about that book

that you couldn't wait another week to check it out?"

"It. . . it was because of Charlie," Billie mumbled.

"Charlie?"

"My brother. I'm trying to teach him to read, and he likes horses." Billie stopped. His words came breathlessly. He couldn't stand what she thought of him. "The book might not be there next week."

"Surely he'll learn to read just as well as you do when he starts school, Billie," she said. "You don't have to teach him yourself."

"He didn't go to school," Billie said. "He's never going to learn unless I teach him."

Mrs. Kelly looked at him intently. "How old is Charlie?"

"Thirteen."

"And he can't come to school?"

"No. He'd never come now with all the little kids. Besides, he works the vegetable fields."

Mrs. Kelly stood so still for so long that it made Billie worry. Maybe she was going to send out a posse or something to bring Charlie in. Maybe he shouldn't have told. Maybe there was a law now that all Indian children had to go to school just like other Florida children.

"You know, Billie," she said at last. "The words in *Misty* are really too hard for someone who is just beginning. I'm afraid Charlie might get very discouraged, or else end up memorizing the sentences, and that wouldn't be reading at all. If you'll stay after school a little while this afternoon, I'll collect some things for you from the first grade teacher. All right?"

He stared up at her. She had said nothing at all about punishment.

"I'd. . . I'd like that," he said, and he smiled at her, a full appreciative smile, the way Charlie would if he could.

At three, when he went up to her desk, Mrs. Kelly had a box of flash cards. There were letters of the alphabet on some and combinations of letters on others, which made certain sounds. One card said, "at," and Mrs. Kelly showed Billie how he could put other letters in front of "at" to make "hat" or "sat" or "cat." Slowly she explained the procedure to Billie, and then she did it all again, slowly, carefully. She told him how important it was to go slowly, how important it was to give praise, how important to practice every day, so that Charlie could learn to sound out simple words himself after he had learned the alphabet and the sounds which the letters made.

"Once Charlie knows all the letters and all the words you can make with these, I'll give you more cards and a book that Charlie can keep. Now," she added, standing up, "I know I've made you miss your bus, so I'll drive you home."

She put on her sweater, and they went down to the car, Billie gratefully clutching the flash cards, his head reeling. Maybe Charlie could do it! Maybe he really could!

"I don't know what the superintendent would say if he knew about this," Mrs. Kelly smiled. "We don't usually suggest that our pupils teach their brothers to read. But you're no ordinary person, Billie, and I think there may be something special between you and Charlie—something we don't see too often between brothers. So it's worth a try. Just don't be discouraged if it goes terribly, terribly slowly."

Billie was afraid for a moment that she might park the car and walk back into the camp with him, but she didn't.

"Good luck, Billie," she said, as she let him out at the edge of the highway. "Let me know if any problems develop, and we'll see if we can work them out."

"Okay," Billie grinned, and started to walk away, then turned. "Thanks, Mrs. Kelly. Thanks a lot."

"B," said Charlie. "Buh."

"Right. You're doing fine," said Billie. "What's this one?"

"N?"

"Huh uh."

"M?"

"Good. What sound does it make?"

"Uh. . . Mmmm?"

"Hey, Charlie, you're doing great!"

Charlie shrugged and leaned against one post of the chickee. "Doesn't sound like words to me."

"You have to get the sounds of the letters first and then we'll put them together," Billie promised. "We've got time. Got the whole year."

"Didn't know we had a teacher in the family," Tiger said from across the chickee where he was working on a new belt for himself.

"It's a good thing, too," put in Mush Jim. "If you're going to live in the white man's world, you've got to know how to get along in it, and you can't get along very well if you can't read."

"No one learns the Mikasuki tongue any more," said Abraham. "The stories of our people, the dances, the medicine—they die with the old and will be lost."

"It's a new world, Father," Mush Jim said. "The Indian does not lie still and wait to be kicked. No longer does he go where he is pushed and settle for what's left over. An Indian today can be a lawyer. He can go to school and learn the books and argue for his people in the courts. He can make people listen. The new Indian knows his rights, and he will not let them be taken from him. Let Billie and Charlie become more than Tiger and me, if they can."

Tiger buffed the belt on the edge of his boot and gave a sharp laugh. "You make it sound so easy for them, Jim. All they've got to do is learn to read the white man's books and they'll be able to solve our problems. They'll be able to get the government to give us back our land and homes and horses. I do not want my sons to hope for the stars and get only a handful of sand. Prepare them to live in the world as it is. Teach them only what is possible for the red man. Don't let their hope get any bigger than an acorn or a stone."

Billie's heart sank down to his feet. When Tiger talked this way, Billie just wanted to go away—to get in the dugout canoe and row far out in the lagoon where only the frogs would sing to him. When

Father took his hope away, there wasn't anything left. He did not like this kind of talk.

Abraham shook his head. "I envy nothing of my white brother. Nothing does he have which I want. It is he who envies me. It is he who travels my rivers, hunts in my forests. But he looks and looks and never finds. He is never at peace with the forest. He is never at peace with himself. He does not know how to be an Indian."

Billie's head swam. Three different Mikasuki men, and they all had different ideas about what it meant to be Indian. He wondered if Charlie were feeling as confused as he was.

It was Charlie who broke the tension. "All I want right now is to learn the alphabet," he said, "and already you're talking about me arguing cases in court."

Tiger and Mush Jim chuckled, and Billie grinned too. If Charlie never learned to read, maybe his sense of humor would help him get by!

"Hush!" came the voice of Sihoki. "Listen!" All eyes turned to look where Grandmother was pointing. There on the roof of the cookhouse sat an owl. With pounding hearts they waited. Maybe it would fly away. But then the owl hooted, and everyone knew that it was bad luck if an owl hooted from the roof of one's house.

"Ei!" cried Grandmother. "Misfortune is on the way!"

"We should have even more after the hurricane takes our home from us?" Abraham quipped. "The owl thinks of something worse than that we should live almost upon the highway itself?"

Yet all believed, some more than others. Abraham grew quiet, and Alice Tommie hugged Watsie in her arms as though the little girl herself were in danger. The next day went by and the next, and nothing happened. Billie forgot the omen of the hooting owl until he got home from school one Friday and was told that Sihoki had broken her arm. She had fallen on her way to wash clothes.

Mush Jim and Alice had taken her to the hospital, and Watsie was alone with Grandfather.

Abraham could tell Billie very little. He did not know what would happen to his wife or how long she would be there. He sat silently in his chickee, pipe in his hands, but unlit. When Sihoki was gone, part of Abraham went also.

Things were happening too fast for Grandfather. The new camp, so close to the highway, was never home to him. The trucks at night kept him awake. The sun here was too bright, the day sounds too close and hard and metallic. Only Sihoki linked him somehow with the life they had enjoyed before, and now she was gone.

"She'll be back tomorrow, Father," Alice Tommie said consolingly. "Here now, taste the meat. I've made it especially for you." She coaxed him into eating a few bites, but it did not taste as it did when Sihoki made it.

"How was she feeling when you left her?" Tiger asked.

"Better, I think. They gave her something for the pain, and she was sleepy. But they want to take another x ray before she comes home, and it will be a long time before she can use her arm. I will not let her do the washing again. The bank is too steep. She will break a leg the next time."

Abraham sat quietly, listening. The bank of their old island home had sloped gently, with no sharp rocks to fall against. Sihoki had no trouble there.

"It will be hard for her with nothing to do," Alice went on. "She will not be able to sew or cook, and time will pass slowly."

It was worse than anyone had imagined, however. Sihoki arrived home on Sunday afternoon like a bobcat which had been dipped in cold water. She was furious at the long hard cast on her arm. She was furious at the hospital, the nurses, the doctors, and the monster-bed with sides on it that bounced her around like a feather in a windstorm every time she turned over.

When she got her breath, she sat down on a bench beside Abraham and fanned herself with her one free hand. The indignity of it all!

First they had taken her clothes away and given her nothing but a stiff white tent to wear all night long. They had taken off her necklaces and put a cellophane bracelet on her arm, and when the nurse brought the necklaces back the next morning and dressed her again, she put them on all wrong.

The nurse had jabbed her with a needle. The doctor had twisted and turned her arm till she thought he was trying to break it even more. The food they gave her was fit only for pigs—soup with nothing in it, and some horrible thing called spaghetti. And all the while, the woman in the bed next to her was watching the television which was hooked onto the wall so high that Sihoki couldn't turn it off even if she'd known how. And just when she drifted off to sleep the next morning, exhausted, the nurse came in with a little glass stick to put in her mouth and a rubber pump to tie on her arm, thoroughly awakening her again.

"Abraham," she said at last, stopping for breath, "what is it they tell me? You do not eat?"

"It is all right now that you are back," he told her, but still his dinner went untouched.

Billie put aside the flash cards that evening and sat with Grandfather instead.

"Sihoki said once that sometimes animals speak and stones move, Grandfather. Is that true?" Billie asked, hoping for a story.

But Grandfather did not feel like telling stories tonight. Besides, no one took them seriously any more. No one believed, and therefore, no one saw or heard the things that might be.

"I do not feel like talk," he said at last, putting one hand on Billie's knee. "But I will listen. It is good that you talk to me. You are like a babbling brook, always moving, always talking, keeping an old man's ghost from wandering away."

Ten

NOVEMBER became December, and December, January. The cold seemed more penetrating somehow in the new camp. The trees were less thick, the water more open, and the cold spells which gripped Florida in the winter, damaging the citrus crop, seemed to settle deep in Abraham's bones. He put on more clothes than he used to and stayed in the cookhouse longer.

It was the hunting season, and often the early morning air was shattered by the crack of a rifle somewhere off in the swamp. Mush Jim, too, went hunting, and then there was rabbit for supper. Sometimes white hunters paid him to be their guide.

February arrived, and with it, frost. The wind blew from the north, and campfires burned low. The tips of the tall grass turned brown, and the cypress and scrub oak shed their leaves. The rest of the landscape turned a pale green, as though winter had sucked the very color from the plants. Sheets of canvas were attached to the sides of the chickees to keep out the rain and the cold.

Grandfather amused himself and the others with the stories he had told so often before. Winter was a good time to talk about the mischievous little manlike dwarfs that lived in the ground and the mythical serpents that roamed the swamps. He told Billie that when the moon was eclipsed, it meant that a toad frog had come along and eaten away at the moon's surface until it completely disappeared. When he was a small boy, Abraham said, he remembered how his people had shot off guns and raised a great cry when the sun or moon was being eaten by the frog.

All this made the long dark evenings in camp go by faster, but it did not make them any warmer.

Alice Tommie began to talk about a hookup to a power line. Other Indians had electricity and were able to have refrigerators and television sets in their chickees. It would be nice, she mused. They could even have an electric heater.

Jeff Miller continued to visit, but he did not stay overnight in the cold months.

"That's how you guys live so long—you sleep outdoors all the time," he kidded. "Man, don't you just about freeze, Billie? There was frost last night. I was cold at home with a mattress and four blankets!"

"Thick blood," said Billie, pounding his chest, not knowing the answer himself. But it was true about the Seminoles being long-lived.

Nonetheless, the family worried about Sihoki. The arm was not healing as it should, and now she seemed to be getting arthritis in it as well. No one spoke it aloud, but they all began to wonder if she would ever be able to use it much again. The inactivity made her crabby, and her crossness upset Grandfather. Nothing seemed quite the same any more.

Abraham began talking again about a return to the old island. He missed the spotted skunk and the quail, the kites and the kingfishes. He longed for the flesh of the land turtle and the taste of sassafras in the spring. "Let us go back where we have grown up as herbs of the woods," he said to Sihoki. If she could never use her arm again, then he would gather the wood and do the cooking himself. And if the spirits of her ancestors called her home, then her last days would be happy ones back on the far island.

The idea of electricity in the chickee bothered them both. Soon there would be talk of moving into a trailer, perhaps, or even a cinderblock house, one of those boxes with holes to see out. Perhaps it was time for the old people to go live by themselves. The island was close enough that Mush Jim could drop by every day or so to make sure nothing was wrong. It was close enough for Charlie and Billie to come by when they gigged for frogs, and the dog could go back to live with them and keep them company.

"I'll take you back to the island on Thursday, Father," Mush Jim promised. "We'll look over the place and see what we can do. I'm sure we can build back two chickees at least."

"They'll be happier in the old place," Alice Tommie said to Tiger that evening. "I can see it in Father's eyes. He never wanted to live here. They will plant another garden and the dog will follow them about, and they will be happy. But it is better the rest of us stay here, for Charlie and Billie especially."

Billie sat in the cookhouse listening, almost too numb to breathe. What he had feared the most was upon them: Grandfather was going away. He had not thought that Abraham really would. He had not thought they would let him. But slowly, as one thing happened on the heels of another, the inevitable had been taking shape. The family was dividing between young and old, and now each would go a different way.

Again Billie felt the impulse to pack up and go along. He would chop the fire wood, draw the water, chase the chickens from the garden, fish and hunt, and learn to use the adz. Life would be as it had always been before. Night would follow day and day would follow night. Spring would follow winter, then summer and fall. Grandfather would tell him stories, and the Indian lore of centuries past would close in around them as the evening shadows fell. Like Abraham, he felt a yearning for all the things man could never make.

And yet, however much he loved the far island, it was nice now being able to walk over to Mush Jim's boat shack whenever he liked—nice to have Jeff come by after school—nice to be able to walk down the highway, to get a Coke at the Indian Village and to talk to the other boys who gathered there. He was a part of this world too—of noise and movement and action. He hung around the gas station and talked to the drivers who drove from Miami to Naples, from Tampa to Key West. They let him sit in the cab of the big semi-trailers, gave him nickels, and joked. They told him about places he had never been, things he had never seen. All this he would miss if he moved back to the island, and he felt that his heart belonged in two places. For days he hung wretchedly around his grandfather, saying nothing.

Then, on Tuesday, two things happened to Billie that somehow seemed very important. First, at school, Mr. Bernard told him that the science class would be dividing into several groups for a unit on conservation. Each group would have a leader, and he wanted Billie to lead a group studying forest conservation. They were to make charts and maps, posters and murals. They could even write a play if they wished, and at the end of six weeks, they were to present a program to the rest of the class, teaching them all that they had learned. Would he do it?

Can I? Billie wondered instantly. And instantly, the Mikasuki ancestors whispered to him, "Who is more capable than you? Which sons of the white men have loved the earth as long as we? Which of them holds all life with the same reverence? Can you, who have so much to give, say no?"

"Sure, I'll do it." Billie answered, his head swimming with excitement.

"Good. I know I can count on you to do a fine job," Mr. Bernard said.

That was the first important thing that happened. Then, as Billie left the bus stop that afternoon and started for Mush Jim's shack, a small truck stopped on the edge of the road, and Mr. Miller leaned out the window.

"Just the fella I want to see," he said. "Next week some of the volunteers from the Wildlife Federation are going to make a tour of Big Cypress and check the water flow—see if we can avoid those floods we had last year. I'm going to take Jeff along—give him an idea of the kind of work we do. I wondered if you'd like to come too? Maybe give you a taste of being a ranger, in case you're ever interested."

"Sure!" Billie said for the second time that day, and again the Mikasuki ancestors inside him whispered, "Who is more capable than you? Who knows better where the animals hide and how the waters flow and when the winds are strongest?"

When Billie reached the camp that afternoon, he was bursting with news. The spirits of his ancestors were right. He had much to give, much to teach, and who would he teach if he stayed hidden on the far island?

Abraham listened silently, but when Billie had finished, he nodded his head. "You will do well, Billie," he said. "You have the wisdom of the Mikasuki behind you."

When Thursday afternoon came, Mush Jim and Abraham got in the airboat to ride back to the old island. They would clean the debris from the clearing, and later, the relatives would build two chickees.

"Want to come, Billie?" Mush Jim called, but Billie was busy working on a poster for school. Halfway through the afternoon, he got tired, so he took a dime for the candy machine and started out for the gas station. There were no trucks that interested him this time, however, and no people he wanted to meet. He got the candy and came back home, listening to the crunch of his solitary footsteps on the dry grass. He was surprised to find his uncle back in camp already.

"Thought you were going to work on the island," he said, lifting the *sofkee* spoon and drinking some of the gruel. And when he got no answer, he turned and looked at his uncle. "What's the matter?"

"Bad luck. Hunters have built a shack there and are using the island for a camp. We've no rights. It's theirs as much as ours. They couldn't have known we were coming back some day."

"But. . . what about Grandfather?" Billie began, looking over at Abraham.

The old man sat silently in his chickee, hands on his knees. There was nothing he wanted to say.

When Billie got up Friday morning, Grandfather

was still sitting in the same place, for he hadn't slept at all. Nor did he eat breakfast.

"We'll just have to find another island," Mush Jim said, shaving at the little mirror tacked to a post. "I know how you feel, Father. Soon as I get a chance, I'll try to see if I can find another place not too far away."

There were none that were as close to them as the old island, Billie knew. They'd looked before. Now his grandparents would have to move even farther away, or live out their lives by the Tamiami Trail.

"Grandfather," Billie said suddenly, sitting down by the old man, "I think I'll stay home today. You said you had a song to teach me."

"No, Billie," Grandfather said, and his eyes crinkled a little. "You go to school, for you are Charlie's teacher as well. You must learn many things about the white man's world."

"You didn't go to school and you made out okay," Billie reminded him. "You never tried to be one of the 'new Indians'."

"New Indian, old Indian—all the same," Grandfather replied. "The true Indian is a man who remembers the ways of his forefathers, even in the white man's world, who does not step on his brother to get more for himself. You go now. Tonight I will teach you the new song, maybe."

Billie was restless at school that day. He felt as the dog did before a storm—edgy, uncertain, moody. The dog had been restless that morning also, whining as Billie and Charlie and Tiger left the camp.

"Be still," Tiger had commanded as they left, but it didn't seem to help. The dog followed them down to the pickup truck across the canal and then slunk back across the footbridge, tail between his legs.

Billie returned the set of flash cards, for Charlie had learned them well, and Mrs. Kelly gave him a new set of more difficult words and combinations. She also gave Billie a book to give to Charlie, an easy reader called, *A Horse, Of Course*, and it was funny. Not exactly the kind of horse book Charlie had in mind, but better than flash cards, and Charlie was getting eager to go faster.

"He'll like this, Mrs. Kelly," Billie said. "Thanks a lot."

"He deserves it, Billie," she answered, and her smile was relaxed and friendly.

It should have been a good day. He should have felt great about the book for Charlie. Instead, Billie sat off by himself at recess, watching the time, and was the first one on the bus at three o'clock. He got off at the usual stop, and followed the canal to the footbridge.

The first thing he heard was the dog's long, penetrating whine, like an animal in a pen wanting to be set free. And then another sound seemed to cut right through his skin—a low, shaky moan of an old woman. Again the dog howled and again Sihoki moaned, and Billie leaped over the footbridge, pushed his way through the grass, and ran into camp, flinging his books on the ground.

He could see Abraham's silhouette against the sky, sitting just where he'd been that morning. Sihoki lay in a heap beside him. Billie had never heard such terrible cries from his grandmother. Before he could speak, Alice Tommie came over quickly. She put her arms around Billie and held him tightly to her.

"What is it?" Billie asked, alarmed. "Has Grand-mother fallen again?"

There were tears on his mother's cheeks. "Mush Jim has gone to get your father and Charlie," she answered. "It is Abraham. Your grandfather is dead."

As though the sun had set, never to rise again above the cypress trees. As though the wolf and panther had left the forest, never to tread again on the soft pine needles. As though the limpkin was crying his heart out above the wide lagoon, and marsh rabbits wept in the saw grass. Grandfather was dead.

Billie pushed away from his mother, not because he didn't want her—he just didn't believe her. Not Grandfather! Sihoki, maybe—that he would believe when it happened, but not Grandfather. Abraham was supposed to live until he was one-hundred at least, maybe a hundred and fourteen. He couldn't go now. It wasn't true. Only that morning he'd said he had a song. . . .

Billie made his way slowly across the ground to the chickee where Grandfather sat. The old man's body leaned a little to one side now, in the same position Billie had left him that morning. The face was turned strangely up toward the sun, and the eyes were closed, as if squinting.

"Grandfather," whispered Billie, leaning toward him.

But the lips did not move, the hands remained

fixed, the eyes stayed closed. Billie turned away, rested his head against a post, and wept without a sound.

A squeal of tires came from the other side of the canal. A door slammed, then another, and there were footsteps across the footbridge, coming through the grass. Mush Jim and Tiger and Charlie came over to the chickee. Billie felt a hand on his shoulder and looked up at his father.

"It's not too late, is it?" he wept, already knowing. "Can't you get a medicine man to bring him back?"

"The medicine men are old now, Billie," Tiger said. "Abraham's ghost has gone. Let it go in peace."

Another head touched Billie's, and Charlie, too, leaned against the post and cried. He kept his mouth open so that sobs could escape, and every so often took in a big gasp of air.

Slowly the round heap at Abraham's feet rose up. With her one good arm, Sihoki unloosened her hair till it fell loose around her shoulders like a long black cape. Strand by strand, she removed her beads. Abraham's soul had reached the east, and there was no calling it back.

Grandfather was to be buried in the old way. Lovingly, his body was dressed in his best clothes, the long shirt of yellow and blue flowers with the green kerchief around his neck. Gently, the body was placed in a handmade casket of rough boards and carried to the dugout canoe.

With Watsie in her arms, Alice Tommie went down

to the canoe to say good-bye to her father. When she came back, Sihoki went alone. The old woman's lips were etched with a thousand wrinkles, and the folds under her eyes each seemed to bespeak a tragic event in her life—the death of a child, a hurricane, a fire in the saw grass, a drought—but today the lines seemed deeper than ever. Slowly she moved through the trees, her long hair flowing around her, until she reached the canoe, where she stooped down, and her shoulders shook. Ordinarily, a widow went with her dead husband into the forest to mourn for several days, but Sihoki was too old and too feeble.

There were no tears on her face when she came back, and her lips were pressed firmly together. The Seminoles accepted death as they accepted the birth of a baby. It was as natural as the blooms on the saw grass, as inevitable as the sunset.

"Now it is time," Sihoki said. Mush Jim and Billie got in one end of the canoe and Tiger and Charlie in the other, and began their silent journey across the water. They were heading southward, far beyond the island where the old camp had been, beyond the hunters even. They would travel until they found a small island deep in the heart of the Everglades. No one talked. The shadows lengthened as the sun went down beyond the mangrove swamp, and still they pressed on to the place where they would build Abraham's last chickee.

Billie watched the ripples as the oars slashed the water. The small heads of snakes rose above the surface, gliding along with the boat. An occasional alligator watched them pass with unmoving eyes, and dragonflies fluttered and touched down on the water in their silent evening dance. Down narrow water trails they went, barely wide enough for the canoe, past coontie and china brier, wild plums and sea grapes.

For eighty years this had been Abraham's home—Abraham of the Panther Clan, Abraham the canoe maker, chickee builder, farmer, chicken tender, pig raiser, woodcarver, fisherman, story-teller. And now he was gone, as softly as a breeze passes by on a summer day, as gently as the sleeping canopy flutters in an evening wind.

Grandmother would never go to another camp now, but would move about with the family wherever they went, no matter how she felt about it. Mush Jim and Father would probably lose interest in the Green Corn dance now that Abraham was not here to go with them. Charlie was learning to read, and Watsie would soon be talking. Perhaps Mother would get electricity, and maybe there would even be a mailbox on the post by the footbridge some day. This was why the dead had lured Grandfather on, Billie knew, and why no one could call him back. The world had changed too much.

It was almost dark when the canoe bumped the bank of a distant island, hidden so well among the trees and saw grass that Billie hardly knew it was there.

Each carried a load up the bank, and helped clear a place for the casket. With colored powder, Tiger made a black spot on Abraham's left cheek and a red spot on his right. Mush Jim put a small piece of burnt wood in Abraham's left hand and a small bow in the right. The casket was placed on the ground with Grandfather's feet to the east, so that when his spirit rose up, it would be heading toward the path in the sky. A chickee of sorts was built over it, a single log for the roof.

It was time to put inside the casket all the things that Abraham had loved. Billie picked up the old man's pipe, broke it in half, and placed it in the coffin. Charlie took his dinner pan, bent it, and put it there also. Tiger broke Abraham's rifle, and Mush Jim chipped the cup from which Grandfather drank his coffee. The bending and breaking of all Abraham's possessions released the spirit of each, and they would all go with the old man on his long journey. When this was done, Mush Jim closed the lid of the casket and placed food and water beside it to nourish Abraham on his way.

Two holes were dug at each end of the coffin, and fires built in each. For four days, Mush Jim would travel back alone to see that the fires were still going, and then neither he nor anyone else in the family would ever go there again.

With the two fires glowing in the blackness like the red eyes of a panther, the family went back to the bank and slipped away.

Billie looked out over the dark water. It was strange, but somehow it seemed as though Grandfather were still in the canoe and going back home along with them. Who could say that Grandfather was gone when they repeated his stories around the fire on a chilly February night? Who could say he was gone when they hunted with the bow and arrows he had made for them, drank from the bowls he had carved, glided in the canoe he had built with his own hands? Who could say he was gone when they sang the songs he had taught them, when the dog crept to the spot in the chickee where the old man had sat, when Sihoki cried out his name in the middle of the night beneath her muslin canopy?

A rush of wind over the water seemed like a loud whisper from all of the Mikasuki ancestors together, and a sudden surge of courage crept into Billie's sadness. Grandfather's spirit would never die as long as Billie kept it alive. Wasn't that what being a true Indian was all about—keeping alive the spirits which had gone on before? And if he could teach the white men also, wouldn't that be even better? If he could work in the white man's world and speak the white man's language and teach the white man what the Indian way was all about, wouldn't that be the best thing he could do for Grandfather?

The canoe glided out from under the lacy branches of the cypress and headed for deeper water, as the sky opened wide above them.

Billie looked up and drew in his breath sharply. The Milky Way spread clear and bright, more brightly than he had ever seen it. Surely Grandfather would find it now—that city in the sky—for the stars spilled out like a million fireflies on a moonless night to welcome a true Indian home.